Seasons

Gail Gaymer Martin

Heartsong Presents

A note from the author:

I love to hear from my readers! You may correspond with me by writing:

Gail Gaymer Martin
Author Relations
PO Box 719
Uhrichsville, OH 44683

ISBN 1-57748-477-0

SEASONS

All of the characters and events in this book are fictitious. Any resemblance to actual persons, living or dead, or to actual events is purely coincidental.

Cover illustration by Victoria Lisi and Julius.

PRINTED IN THE U.S.A.

prologue

The icy February wind penetrated her body. The canvas flapped overhead, and a distant voice drifted in and out of her hearing. She felt numb, numb through to her heart. The canvas flapped loudly again. Suddenly the voice stopped. A hand reached under her elbow to help her from the cold metal chair. The heel of her shoe turned in a rut in the frozen earth. Her legs buckled.

"Are you okay?" someone asked, grabbing her arm to steady her.

Even in the icy cold, the heavy scent of dying flowers caught on the wind and filled her nostrils. Her stomach churned. Well-wishers patted her arm, her shoulder. Words, sad words, floated into her consciousness—*so sorry. . .with God. . .deepest sympathy*—words she didn't want to hear.

She didn't want sympathy. She wanted Tim. She wanted to scream out, to close her eyes so it would all go away. She tried to make it go away continually, ever since she received the call. *Michigan State Police. . .accident. . .hospital. . .serious*. These, too, were words she didn't want to remember.

Someone nudged her back, or was it the wind? She wanted to strike out and cry, "Let me alone. I can't leave him here." Tears rolled down her icy cheeks—warm tears, the only warmth left in her.

"Come on, Sally. It's too cold to stand here. Let's get into the car," her brother's voice urged—softly distressing her. She knew he was trying to help, but no one could.

She found herself moving through the patches of crusted

snow toward the sleek black limousine. Heat met her face as the door opened, and she leaned over to slide in. The door closed. A gust of cold air announced the opening of another door. Bill, her brother, and his wife, Sue, climbed into their seats. The door closed. Sally felt the vehicle move slowly along the gravel road, heading back to the church for a luncheon prepared for the mourners. She was a mourner, but she didn't want to eat. She wanted to stay here with Tim.

Her eyes were drawn back to the flapping canvas, the mound of flowers, the hard earth camouflaged with artificial grass, and the bronze box holding inside her love. Her husband. Her heart.

one

"Enough is enough."

Sally Newgate chided herself as the church steeple loomed into view. She shook her head, bringing herself back to the present, and turned her coupe into the parking lot of Holy Cross Church. Each week old memories tugged at her as she participated in the support group. At her first session, Jack Holbrook opened the program with a reading from Ecclesiastes, "To every thing there is a season, and a time to every purpose under the heaven." She hadn't believed it at first, but now, she'd begun to.

When Sally entered the Fellowship Hall, she searched the rows for a familiar face, and spying one, she slid in next to the woman, pulling a notebook from her handbag. "Ready?"

The woman flashed her own pad and pencil. "Sure am." She turned an embarrassed grin toward Sally. "Before I started these meetings I thought I was the only one with troubles."

Sally grinned. "You're not alone. You're surrounded by multitudes." She gestured toward the growing crowd sitting around the large hall. As her gaze followed her arm's sweep of the room, her smiling face lifted, and she looked into the friendly chocolate-brown eyes of Brad Mathews.

He stood above her, his ashen hair falling in a soft wave with one curl dipping to his forehead. "Thanks for the welcoming smile." He looked amused. "It was for me, wasn't it?"

Sally felt a blush creep along her hairline. Mesmerized by his sparkling eyes, she stared at him without a word. Brad had edged his way into her thoughts since the day they met. For so long, memories of Tim filled every moment of her day. But lately, the pain had softened and settled into acceptance.

"Sorry," he said finally. "I was trying to step by without disturbing you—to sit there." He pointed to the chair next to Sally. "Now I'm waiting, hoping you'll invite me to join you."

Sally fluttered. "Goodness. You don't have to ask. Please join us." Words tumbled out, and she swallowed to gain control of a rush of emotions. From the first session, Sally had found him attractive. But tonight, dressed in beige slacks and a heather green pullover, he looked strikingly handsome. His gaze stayed connected to hers, and she felt her flush deepen.

His full lips curved into a bright smile. "Thanks for the invitation." He stepped past her and slid into the chair.

The chatter subsided as Jack stepped to the microphone. "Tonight our topic is 'A Time to Keep and a Time to Throw Away.' For each of you, the time of grief is different. Some of you have made changes in your lives. Some haven't. It doesn't mean you love more or less than the next person. It only means that your adjustment to the change has proceeded more quickly or more slowly. That's all."

His words flooded into Sally's memory. She recalled a year and a half earlier when she wasn't ready to remove Tim's belongings from her bedroom. She had wandered to the closet, cradling his clothing in her arms like a baby, her face buried deep within the cloth. She was stronger now.

When Jack finished his presentation, she headed for the refreshment table, and Brad joined her. Thoughtfully, he pulled a cookie from the tray as if lost in thought. "I wish my kids understood what Jack said. It's difficult to explain to two young children why their mother died. She was active and healthy, and in less than two months, she was gone."

Sally twinged.

"I tried to be brave for them," he continued, "and I suppose the charade was good for me. My kids—that's another story."

"It doesn't matter how old you are," Sally said. "I still miss my mom, and she died ten years ago when I was twenty-four. How long has it been since your wife died?"

"Just over a year. I know it takes time."

Brad's gaze caught hers, and her heart skipped double-time.

The conversation continued into the small group discussion, and when the session ended, Sally headed toward the exit. Brad's long strides brought him to her side, and they left the building into the crisp night, the fall leaves smoldering piles along the curb.

As they ambled down the sidewalk, Sally glanced at him. "I wonder if you should talk more about your wife to your children instead of avoiding it. They'll see you haven't forgotten her, and it gives them permission to talk about her, too."

He slowed to a stop, his hands deep in his pockets, his head bowed. "I do avoid talking about Janet. I'm always afraid I'll make them sadder than they already are." His gaze rose to hers. "What you said makes sense. Thanks."

They continued through the parking lot and reached Sally's car. Brad stood by her side as she opened the door. She paused uncomfortably before sliding in. "Well. . .good night."

His hand rested on the handle. "Thanks for the idea. Good night." He closed her door, hurrying toward his own car.

&

The telephone rang, pulling Sally from a near nap. She dragged herself in a daze across the living room and picked up the receiver, her "hello" a near whisper.

"Sally Newgate?" a glib masculine voice asked.

"Yes. May I ask who's—"

"Hi, it didn't sound like you. This is Steve Wall."

An uneasy feeling ran through her. Steve Wall? From work? Why was he calling?

"Did I wake you?" he asked.

No way would she admit she had fallen asleep on a Saturday afternoon. "No, I was daydreaming, I guess."

She heard a slight chuckle. "That's why I'm calling. I've been daydreaming about you."

Daydreaming? What? His words sent a chill through her. She hardly knew this man.

"Is something wrong? Did I call at a bad time?"

"I'm sorry, Steve," she muttered. "I'm not sure I understand." She clutched the receiver with icy hands. Since Tim's death, the only men who called Sally were related or old, not a man daydreaming about her.

"I'll be blunt. I wondered if you'd have dinner with me sometime. How's that for being more direct?" His voice lifted with good humor. "Next Saturday?"

Sally blanched. She took a deep breath, calming herself. This was ridiculous. "Sorry, Steve. I have plans next weekend." Her niece, Carrie, was to spend the day with her. Though her alibi was real, she decided to be blunt. "I'm rather new at being single, Steve. I'm not dating yet."

Steve's tone took a sarcastic edge. "Mine won't be your only invitation, I'm sure. I can't believe I'm the first to ask you out. You're a lovely woman, Sally. Some other time then?"

Sally hesitated. She pulled the telephone away from her ear, but she stopped herself from hanging up. "Perhaps," she heard herself say, not believing her own voice.

"All right then." His toned brightened. "See you at work."

Sally clutched the telephone, startled more at her reaction than at the call. Placing the receiver on the cradle, she thought of her meetings. She felt terribly disappointed in herself. Shouldn't she be beyond the point of pure panic by now?

Two years had passed. But she still struggled at times feeling Tim let everyone down, dying at thirty-seven. For so

long, Sally felt angry at him. Really, she had been angry at
everyone—the drunk driver, Tim, and even God. Eventually,
her anger turned to sadness, then to loneliness, and now to a
periodic dull ache.

She turned and caught her pale reflection in the hall mirror. Steve had called her attractive. "Lovely," in fact. She
studied her reflection. Her weight-loss, after Tim's death,
defined her cheekbones. Her chestnut hair, then lifeless, had
recaptured its natural sheen. Tim had often told her she was
beautiful. She hadn't heard that word in a long time—or the
word "lovely" for that matter.

&

On Monday, Sally pulled into her driveway after work and
found her neighbor Ed Washburn with a wheelbarrow full of
compost, mulching the perennials in her flower beds. Sally
parked her car and ambled across the grass toward him. He
leaned on the shovel, his white hair contrasting with his
leathery skin.

"Ed, you did this last year for me. I certainly didn't expect
you to do it again."

Ed's hazel eyes crinkled at the edges. "Decided to have the
fun myself." He brushed his white hair off his brow with the
back of his gloved hand. "Really, I finished mulching and
had compost left in the barrow."

"Well, you're the best friend in the world. Thanks."

Sally eyed her flower beds, now tidy with mounds of the
dark earth protecting the lifeless foliage. "You're almost
finished?"

"Yep. This is the last rosebush."

"Come in for a cup of hot tea. I might even find a snack
for you." She elbowed him playfully.

"You know how to get to an old man's heart." Ed grinned.

Ed moved the wheelbarrow and shovel to the edge of the

driveway, then followed Sally to the back door and into the kitchen. He thoughtfully removed his shoes and draped his jacket on a chair as he sat at the oak table by the bay window.

Sally reached for the dish of scones sitting on the counter as Ed eyed the plate.

"Baked some biscuits, did ya?" Ed asked.

"Griddle scones, like my grandma used to make. They're like a sweet biscuit, browned on a griddle. I made these with dried Michigan cherries. I'll warm them for you."

As she talked, she heated the scones and made tea. "Ed, you're a man. Let me ask you something from a male's point of view about being single—dating, actually."

Ed cocked his head, an amused look on his face. "I might be a man, but remember, I'm an *old* man. That's different."

She grinned over her shoulder. "You still had to face being single again after all those years of marriage."

"That's true, but it took me a long time. Alice is the first woman who caught my fancy. Before Alice came along, I still felt married to Mildred. But when I met Alice, I knew. My feelings stirred, and I came alive again."

Sally slid the warm scones and mug of tea on the table. "Here we go."

Ed grabbed up a knife and smoothed butter over the warm pastry. He took a big bite. "These are great."

"I don't make them often. They're too good to be healthy."

Ed laughed and attacked another scone. Sally stood at the counter, sipping her tea, and watched him with pleasure. Sally was amused by the blossoming friendship between Ed and Alice Brown, her elderly church friend. Alice had come to Sally's rescue after Tim's death, full of energy and love, packing and boxing, cleaning and listening—especially listening.

Sally's thoughts drifted back to her question about dating. She looked through the window. The sun's setting rays spread purple and orange across the sky. "A man who works with me called with a dinner invitation, and I fell apart." She refocused on Ed. "You said it earlier. I still feel married."

"When you meet the right man you'll know. You'll feel it inside." Ed tapped his chest. "In your heart. You don't need to look for it either. It'll happen." He chuckled, licking his fingers. "Now, do you need any other words of wisdom from an old man?" He wiped the crumbs from his lips with a napkin.

"No, but thanks." She gazed at his warm smile. "By the way, I've finished decorating my room."

"Well, I'll be. You mean I don't have to listen to you and Alice discuss wallpaper and quilts for a while?" He rose on stiff legs and brushed the crumbs from his lap. "The other day I had a thought. Maybe you'd like an old quilt stand for your room. I could look in the attic. I think there's one there, and you could have it."

"A quilt stand? I'd love to buy one."

"Buy? You already paid me. Those scones were worth a million. The stand belonged to my grandmother. It'll sit up in the attic 'til I die."

"But. . .give it away?"

"What do I want with that old thing? If my son were living, maybe he'd like it, but since he's gone, I'd like you to have it more than anyone."

"Son?" His statement jolted her. "Ed, I had no idea you had a son. How did he die?"

"In Vietnam." He remained silent for a moment. "It was so hard on Mildred. He was our only child."

"You've talked about Mildred, but never about your son."

"I try to think about the good times."

"I wish I'd do that. I'm always moping because we never had a child, and here you had a child who died. That's worse."

"I had him for a time, Sally. I knew him and loved him—and I have memories."

"Memories," Sally repeated, plopping down at the kitchen table. "Memories can be bad."

Ed rested his hands against a chair back. "They're bad at first, maybe. Later on you'll concentrate on the good things."

"Life can be so ironic. I may never be a mother."

"You're still young. You have a whole future ahead of you."

She gazed at his gentle face lined by his own hurts and sorrows. "Do you go to church, Ed? Funny, I don't think I've ever asked you."

A tender grin flickered on his lips. "Mildred and I went every Sunday. After Mildred died, I got out of the habit, I guess. Too lonely. Wouldn't go to bed at night, though, without reading my Bible. It gives me perspective."

"Perspective, that's what I need." She rose and pressed her cheek to Ed's. "You are an amazing man."

"Well now, I think that's a compliment."

&

Brad stood near the refreshment table, focusing on the wall clock. Sally hadn't arrived yet, and disappointment trudged through him. His recurring thoughts of her seemed to be a mixture of pleasure and guilt. Since he first heard her speak in the small group sessions, he couldn't get her out of his mind. What captivated him were her warm, sensitive eyes, the brightest moss green he'd ever seen.

He hadn't looked that deeply into a woman's eyes since Janet died. And he supposed this was what caused his guilt. Janet had always been a sensible woman. If she could speak to him now, she'd say, "Brad you can love my memory, but you can't love me. So don't be foolish. Make a new life for yourself and for the kids. What are you waiting for?" His lips curled into a private grin at the thought of her.

"And what's causing that little, secret grin?"

He looked down into Sally's eyes. She stared at him with curiosity. Again, her gaze left him flustered.

"Just life, I suppose."

Sally remained riveted to him. "Life can be amusing."

"To be honest, I was thinking about Janet." He couldn't admit he was also thinking of her. "If Janet were here, she'd be sending me down the road to get on with it. 'Things will never get better if you just think about them.' Maybe not that exactly, but. . .she'd say my life's on hold."

"Tim, too," Sally said, with a knowing look. "He'd go with the flow, as they say. Not me. I get in the canoe and tip over." Her full, bright lips parted to a smile.

"You do have a gift for words. I've lost my oars many times, too. Especially going over the rapids."

The microphone squealed, and Brad turned to see Jack waiting for the room to quiet. "I suppose we should grab a seat."

Jack opened the meeting with prayer and introduced his topic, "A Time to Seek." Brad felt rattled by Sally's nearness. He recalled about nine months after Janet died, his cousin Darlene invited him to dinner. She hadn't told him she'd also invited a divorced lady friend. He'd made the best he could out of the situation, but in his heart, the evening was a disaster. At work, women dropped hints here and there they were available and interested. The problem was, he wasn't—until now.

Concentrating on the presentation proved difficult. Brad couldn't keep his eyes from Sally. She followed Jack's every move. Her expression reflected Jack's words, her head nodding, her mouth curving into a fleeting grin.

Suddenly, she turned toward Brad with a questioning glance, her skin tone rising to a shy schoolgirl pink. Tender sensations surged through him. Before he could force his attention on Jack, the presentation concluded.

"Jack's right," Sally said. "It's what you said. You can't sit around waiting for life to happen, you have to find a new life, make new friends and new traditions. Sounds easier than it is." She rose, and Brad followed.

"I couldn't help but think of my cousin's good intentions at playing matchmaker. A horrible experience. I wasn't ready at all. Haven't been, yet. Not one date."

Sally's eyes brightened. "Nice to know I'm not alone—and it's been longer for me. A coworker asked me to dinner, and you'd think he asked me to eat worms. I panicked. I disappointed myself."

"Maybe he wasn't the right one." His pulse fluttered as a faint ray of hope rose inside him. "One day it'll happen for both of us." He gazed into her lovely eyes, and his mind filled with images. *Maybe someday you'll like to have dinner with me.*

She smiled, and his stomach took a dive. He prayed he hadn't spoken his thoughts aloud. "Did I say something?"

She grinned. "No, but you sound like my neighbor. He said when the right one comes along I'll know it. In my heart."

"And how old is this neighbor?" His question jokingly hid a real fear.

She looked at him slyly. "About a hundred, maybe."

two

Brad sat in his cousin Darlene's living room, sipping coffee after dinner. Her words filled him with nostalgia, not that their situations were the same, but the loneliness for both of them was real. "Divorce is a little like death, Darlene. I can understand. The loneliness seems endless. Then one day, you realize unless you make a move nothing will change."

Darlene curled her legs beneath her on the sofa. "I know, Brad. But the world marches around in twos. I'm always a third wheel. No one to go with anywhere. I've been out of the loop since Phil and I separated. Now I'm facing divorce, and I prayed so hard we'd work things out."

"Keep praying, Darlene, but don't tell God what you want. Ask Him to do His will."

She pushed her curls away from her ears. "Easier said than done."

"I'm in a dilemma, too. I've met a woman in my group."

Darlene leaned forward, raising her eyebrows, and her face relaxed for the first time that evening. "One woman in particular? Doesn't sound like a dilemma at all. Sounds wonderful, Brad."

"Thanks. It's brand-new. No dates, only talking, but I sense something special. I haven't felt that way since Janet—"

"I know, Brad. I can only imagine how I'll feel when my bitterness fades, and I spot that special someone."

Brad rested his elbows on his knees. "But along with the pleasure and anticipation of being with her, I feel guilty."

"Guilty? You knew Janet better than I did, and I know

she'd laugh at you. You can't bring her back. And she'd want you and the kids to be happy."

"It's the kids that bother me. Kelly's having an awful time."

"I can't help you there. I know nothing about kids. Wish I had a couple. They might make my lonely world a little fuller."

"And much more painful," Brad added, shaking his head. Kelly and Danny's hurt faces soared through his mind.

"I suppose you're right."

"Well, anyway, getting back to my new friend. She's witty, compassionate, pretty as a picture, and a Christian. I'll never forget that night, remember, when you invited me for dinner—"

"Please, let's forget that. I felt terrible. Now I know how you felt. I pushed too hard." Her face twisted with the memory.

"Don't feel bad. Look at me now. I'm mooning over a woman I haven't even dated."

"But you've spent time together."

"We have, and she's been helpful with the kids." He paused in thought. "She doesn't have kids herself. I don't know why."

"Maybe she can't. Or thought life was easier without them."

Darlene's words sent an uneasy feeling through him. He couldn't imagine her not wanting kids. "I doubt. . .I suppose I'll find out one of these days." The thought lingered in his mind.

"I'm sure she has her reasons," Darlene said. "I'm glad you met someone, Brad. But if I were giving advice, I'd suggest you move slowly, especially where the kids are concerned. Let them get used to her little by little."

Brad shook his head. "I came over to give you a little support, and instead, you're helping me. I didn't mean that to happen." He leaned against the chair cushion.

Darlene shifted uncomfortably. "Actually, you could help a lot." She paused as if trying to phrase her sentence. "A gal from work invited me to a party, and I hate to go alone. I've sort of hinted my life is normal—with dates. I didn't really lie, but I never admitted I'm a dud."

"You're not a dud."

"No, but I'm alone."

"So you want your old cousin to be your escort, is that it?"

She gave him a flushed smile. "Yeah, and I feel embarrassed. I've never asked a man out before—even my own cousin."

"I'd be happy to take you. And one of these days you'll have lots of dates."

"I'd feel awful if anyone found out who you are." She looked miserable.

"I promise, I won't tell a soul we're related."

"Thanks, pal." She hurried to his side and gave him a hug.

❧

On Thursday at Davidson Electric, Sally sat with Darby in the lunchroom eating a spinach and bacon salad. "I didn't want to say no. Jim so rarely asks me to work overtime, but I don't like working weekends."

"What's up in your department?" Darby wiped her hands on a napkin.

"We're doing some changeovers on our accounts. It's a big job." Sally buttered her roll, glancing around the lunchroom. "I'm so uncomfortable since Steve called. Every time I see him I shudder."

"Don't worry about it."

"I know." Sally finished her salad and slid back the plate. "I want to feel normal, Darby." She paused. "Whatever that is."

"Don't ask me." Darby shrugged.

Sally tapped her fingers on the table. "I wonder if Jim

would mind if I work overtime tonight instead of Saturday?"

Looking at her watch, Darby jumped up. "Wow! Speaking of overtime, our lunch ran overtime. We were due back five minutes ago." They jumped from their seats and hurried back to their desks.

That evening as others left for home, Sally, with Jim's approval, remained behind her computer. When her stomach growled, she looked at the clock, surprised at the late hour. Finishing the final account, she closed the program and turned off the computer.

As she gathered her belongings, a noise resounded in the hallway outside the office. Curiously, she inched open the door. She bolted as a hand darted through the opening to grasp hers. "Aha, so you're here late, too."

Sally recognized Steve Wall's smooth, syrupy voice. She tensed. "Steve, you scared me." Sally forced a casual tone. "You're being dedicated too, huh?"

"I'm not sure it's dedication. It's a necessity for me. If I want to keep my promotion, I work late occasionally."

"If we're confessing, I don't want to work Saturday." She shrugged. "So much for dedication." She hoped to end the conversation. "Well, I'm off. Need to get home and eat. I'm starving." Immediately, she was sorry she set herself up for an invitation.

He took advantage of her lead. "Would you like to stop somewhere? No sense both of us eating alone, is there?"

Sally hesitated. She'd acted like an idiot on the phone and needed to overcome her fears of being single. But she stopped herself. "No, I need to get home, Steve, but thanks."

"Hey, it's only a dinner. No big deal."

Sally ignored his comment and passed him by, heading for the elevator. But he followed. She punched the button and waited.

"I'm sure it's been difficult for you," Steve sympathized. "A woman needs a man around the house for companionship."

He put his arm around her shoulder and Sally shrugged it off. "Most people don't choose to be alone," she stated matter-of-factly, "but I make the best of it. I've learned a lot."

The elevator arrived, and the door slid open. They stepped inside.

"But it's lonely," he whispered, leaning too close to her, "those long nights all alone."

The door shut, and Sally tensed. She felt trapped. "I manage." Her hands trembled, and she placed them in her pockets so he wouldn't notice. "You adjust." Her voice edged with irritation. She lifted her hand, pushing her hair from her face. He moved closer to her, pressing her into the corner. "I'd love to spend some of those lonely nights with you." Steve reached out and grasped at her fingers before she tucked them away. "You're a special woman."

She jerked her hand away from his as the door slid open. Panic rose in her, and she pushed past him into the parking garage. Words tumbled out of her mouth. "I need to get home. I have a busy day tomorrow."

"How about the coffee? Maybe, we could. . ."

Sally wanted to run to her car—to get away from him.

"No, really, I need to get home." She backed away, fear soaring through her.

"Listen, is there some misunderstanding? I didn't mean to chase you away."

Sally halted. "Steve, I'm not looking for a companion. And I'm not desperate for attention. I'm going home."

She turned and darted to her car. She never, ever wanted to be alone with a man again. But as she slid into the driver's seat and locked the door, a gentle, handsome face flashed through her mind.

❧

The following week Brad stood in the foyer of Holy Cross Church and watched Sally hurry through the parking lot. The northern winds blew against her back like an angry crowd pressing her forward. As she reached for the handle, he pulled open the door. She paused, her surprise aimed at him. His heart lurched, and he felt foolish.

The force of the wind whipped against the door, and he propped it open as she literally blew into the foyer.

He waited for her to catch her breath. "Now, that's what we old sea captains on the Cape call a 'nor'easter.' "

She gasped, holding her chest. "I was thinking more of Dorothy and Toto." She ran her fingers quickly through her wind-tossed hair. "You can give me a 'southwester' any day. I assume that's the opposite."

He grinned and walked alongside her as she headed down the hallway. "I suppose you noticed I was waiting for you." His heart thundered with his confession.

She pivoted toward him, her face a sudden pink. "Not really," she said. "But I'm glad you were there."

"I wanted to catch you to say thanks for your idea to talk with the kids about Janet. I've started slowly, but already I see a difference."

"I'm glad."

"I didn't want to confuse them by saying too much, but when it fits, I mention things about her."

"Taking it slow is a good idea."

"I see a look in their eyes now, especially Kelly."

"I suppose not having kids makes it easier for me. But sometimes, I still wish I had one."

Her words brought a smile to his thoughts.

Outside the door of the Fellowship Hall, Brad glimpsed at the easel. "A Time to Heal." The topics always seemed to fit his needs. And fate had nothing to do with it. God knew when he needed a boost.

They wandered in, and Sally gestured toward the refreshment table. "Coffee smells good. I'm chilled through to my bones. Let's have a cup, and I'll tell you about my latest terrible experience."

She headed for the coffee urn, and Brad followed, wondering what she meant. Filling her cup, she began her story, telling him about her experience with Steve in the elevator.

Brad's protective nature rose, but another emotion stirred in him. Jealousy. He didn't want other men forcing their attention on Sally. "Being single again is scary and difficult. The guy's uncaring. He doesn't deserve a second glance."

She shook her head, discouragement showing on her face. "I know, but I feel like a naive school girl. And I guess I don't feel single." She looked directly into his eyes. "But I'll tell you, if I did, I guarantee I wouldn't date Steve."

Her words danced through him. "I suppose, you can't blame the poor guy for trying—especially with a woman, not only attractive, but intelligent and sweet. He couldn't help himself."

He saw her flush shyly, and he couldn't believe himself. The words poured out of him like a leaky bucket. He could have said *attractive* and stopped there. No, he had to add all the other glowing adjectives. She'd assume he was acting like Steve, coming on to her. His thoughts came to a skidding halt. He *was* coming on to her—not very successfully, but that's what he was doing.

Her flush lessened, and she gave him a simpering pout. "He couldn't help himself, hmm? Well, now that you put it that way, I feel sorry for the poor dear. Next time he asks I'll jump at the chance for a date."

He dove in. "You don't have to go that far. I really think the man's a cad." He lay his hand on her arm, and a pleasant sensation ran through him. "Seriously, Sally, don't be hard on yourself. People plug along with grief in stages. But being ready for dating and falling in love—I don't know—that's different."

She nodded. "Maybe, I'm afraid to think about love, because I can be hurt again. Sort of guilty and frightened." Her eyes widened.

She'd put her finger on his feelings.

She looked into his eyes. "I think that's it, exactly," she said, seemingly pleased with herself.

Brad put his arm around her and gave her a quick hug.

She patted his arm, and it wasn't until they found their seats that he realized what had happened—how natural their responses had been. No guilt. No embarrassment. Only warm friendship.

three

Sally stood in her bedroom admiring the quilt stand she and Ed had located in his attic the Saturday before. She had draped it with an old quilt belonging to her mother, and the colors added just the right touch to her newly decorated Victorian room. She smiled remembering last Saturday. Ed wanted to give her the whole attic. From the bottom of a steamer trunk, he had pulled out an old photograph album, bound with a gold clasp and covered in moss green velvet, embossed with darker green vines and small pink blossoms. Sally almost had to stomp her foot to refuse the lovely gift.

She was procrastinating again, she knew. She spent the good part of morning in her bedroom, rummaging through her closet and wondering what to wear to Darby's birthday party. She discovered a simple teal blue dress in the back of her closet. *Tolerable*. She prayed the same word described the party.

Forcing herself into the car, she drove the few miles to Darby's apartment. She felt awful going to her first real party without an escort. Throughout the day she wished she would've had the nerve to invite Brad—like a friend, someone to give her confidence a boost. But she hadn't. The idea was a bit late in coming.

When she arrived at Darby's, she took a deep breath. The door flew open, and a stranger welcomed her in to the spacious, yet crowded, apartment. Darby saw her at the door and hurried across the living room to greet her.

"You're here," Darby said, giving her shoulders a squeeze.

"I'm glad you came. You know lots of people." Darby gestured in the direction of her guests.

Sally nodded, smiling at familiar faces from the office.

The elegant apartment was highlighted by the black teakwood furniture. An abstract art piece in ebony and a copy of a vase from some oriental dynasty caught her eye, displayed in an elegant etagere. As Sally gazed into the cabinet, Eric Farmer, Darby's longtime boyfriend, joined her.

"Hi, Sally."

"Eric, you're so sweet to give Darby this party."

"Can't help myself," he said, guiding her to a table overflowing with hors d'oeuvres. "Can I get you something to drink?"

"Do you have a soft drink?" Sally asked.

"Sure do. I'll be back in a minute."

While Sally waited for him to return, she surveyed the room until she found herself staring into a familiar face.

"Hi, remember me?" he asked, "Ron Morton. We met a long time ago."

"Sure, I thought you looked familiar." Sally gazed again at the handsome man with friendly, deep brown eyes.

"So, how have you been?"

Eric returned with a filled glass, eyeing them together. "I see you two recognized each other."

Sally nodded. "Yes, but it's been a long time."

Eric handed Sally the glass with a wink. "Don't let me interrupt. I'll leave you two alone."

Before Sally could respond, he walked away. His innuendo prompted her to feel self-conscious. They stood, looking at each other in uncomfortable silence.

"I'm not often at a loss for words," she said finally. "Tonight, I'm making my debut as a single—a nervous single."

"Darby mentioned it's your first party." His pleasant smile

revealed a mouth of straight white teeth. "You're doing fine."

Another lull caused Sally further discomfort. "I didn't mean to put a damper on our conversation."

"You haven't, by any means. In fact, I was going to invite you to join me across the room." He gestured to a couple of empty chairs near the fireplace.

Darby swept past them, and Sally's gaze was drawn to the door as she welcomed two latecomers. Sally recognized Darlene Elmwood from the personnel department. But her heart skipped a beat as Brad stepped through the doorway. He greeted Darby with his generous smile and surveyed the room fleetingly. Sally expelled her halted breath. He hadn't seen her.

"Is something wrong?" Ron asked.

Sally pulled herself together, her pulse galloping. "No, I'm fine."

The strange expression on Ron's face forced her to return to their conversation. Moments later, as Darby changed the hors d'oeuvre table to a buffet spread, she excused herself, needing time to regroup.

Sally crossed the room to where Darby was covering a dessert table with a linen cloth. "Can I help?"

Her friend gave her a look of thanks. "The buffet's nearly ready, but I could use help with this table. She handed Sally a pile of plates and silverware. "When you're done with that I have all kinds of goodies in the kitchen."

"Fine, but," she whispered, "do you know the guy who came in with Darlene?"

"No," Darby said, glancing toward the couple. "Why?"

Sally hated to tell her. "He's the man I mentioned from my group meetings."

"Hmm? Nice-looking. Darlene has good taste."

Darby apparently hadn't understood. Sally laid out the dinnerware, pleased to have the distraction, and headed for the

kitchen for the dessert trays. She returned with the large plat-
ters as Darby made room on the table.

When Sally finished, she searched the crowd for Ron, but
her eyes lit on Brad approaching her.

"I couldn't believe it was you." His face beamed, and she
melted with his smile. "What are you doing here?"

She wanted to ask him the same question. "Darby's a
friend of mine." She forced her mouth to curve into a half-
hearted smile, trying to be genial. But what about Darlene?
"I saw you come in. I had no idea you knew Darlene."

His eyes widened, and he paled. "Oh, she's just my c—my
friend." He shifted uncomfortably from one foot to the other.
"We've known each other forever."

His gaze clung to hers, a strange expression creeping across
his face. Sally's heart sank. Obviously he had lied to her.
Never dated before, he had told her. He and Darlene looked
comfortable with each other. This was no first date, she felt
positive.

Disappointment wrestled with anger inside her. He'd lied.
Why? For sympathy or camaraderie? She didn't know. She'd
been fool enough to tell him about Steve as if he would
understand. Brad had played her for a fool, too.

"So, how do you know the hostess?" Brad asked, his pleasant expression wavering. "Or are you here with someone. . .
too?"

He swallowed nervously, and she realized his faux pas had
dawned on him. "No, I'm alone. I told you I hadn't started
dating yet, remember." She stressed the words so forcefully,
she felt embarrassed.

"Me either," he said shifting uncomfortably, ". . .until
Darlene asked me to be her escort. She's separated and hated
to come alone."

"I understand how she feels." She raised her eyes to his

and saw his expression fill with frustration. Despite her anger, she felt sorry for him. He looked miserable.

Before he responded, a hand pressed her shoulder. She turned to face Ron. "I saved your chair if you'd care to join me." He pointed to the empty chairs across the room.

"Thanks, Ron. That would be nice." She wanted to gloat like a hurt child.

Brad scowled.

"Oh, Brad, this is Ron Morton, a friend of mine. Ron, Brad Mathews." She eyed Brad to see his reaction. The scowl remained.

Ron stuck out his hand. "Nice to meet you, Brad." He flashed a look of embarrassment toward Sally. "I hope I didn't interrupt anything here."

She forced an artificial chuckle from her throat. "No, not at all. Brad and I were just chatting." She turned to Brad. "Well, I'll see you next Tuesday, I suppose."

Brad stood wide-eyed. "Right. Tuesday." He turned trance-like and returned to Darlene.

Sally hustled over to the table spread with cold meats and salads, crusty dinner rolls, and pastas. The food looked tasty, but Sally's appetite had vanished. She spooned a few items on her plate and followed Ron across the room. But her mind and eyes were focused on Brad and Darlene.

Brad felt weighted by frustration at the situation. At first, when he saw Sally walking into the kitchen, his heart lifted. He wanted to run to her, pleased he'd agreed to escort Darlene. Then, he realized the ramifications.

The horror of the situation struck him when he looked at Sally's face. She thought he had lied to her. He was sure of it. And he was stuck. He promised Darlene he wouldn't tell anyone she was his cousin. In fact, he'd almost slipped earlier. Darlene turned to him and frowned. "Something wrong?"

"Sort of," Brad said, staring toward Sally. "The woman from my grief group is across the room. The one I told you about." He gestured discretely toward Sally and Ron seated cozily in chairs by the fireplace.

"Well, I'll be," Darlene said. "That's Sally Newgate. She works in accounting."

"I never knew where she worked. I told her I hadn't started dating yet. And now here I am with you. She thinks I lied to her."

Darlene gave him an odd look and shrugged. "She's with a date. What's the problem?"

Brad shook his head. "No, he's not a date. She told me she's alone. I think they just know each other or something."

Darlene chuckled. "Brad, it'll work out. In fact, maybe she lied to you. Maybe he is her date, and she's embarrassed that you caught her. Don't let it ruin your evening."

Her words startled him. "Yeah, maybe," he said, covering his shock. *Sally wouldn't lie to me, would she?* His stomach somersaulted.

Darlene didn't understand. How could she know his feelings? Thoughts of Sally had brightened his days lately and filled him with hope. When Janet died, he believed his world had ended. He knew now he could love again.

He avoided watching her, but when she stopped by the dessert table, he couldn't take his eyes from her. Within minutes, she walked away and headed for the door, pausing a moment to speak with Darby. His stomach lurched when Ron followed. But worse than that, his heart sank when Ron followed her out the door. He had been so certain Darlene was wrong.

❧

When Sally woke Monday morning, the autumn leaves that cluttered the ground were disguised by a thick coating of frost. Sally shivered, realizing winter lurked around the corner. Her thoughts were as icy as the weather. Brad weighed on her mind. She wanted to believe he hadn't deceived her, but she created one scenario after another, and nothing made sense. She longed for Tuesday when she would see him face-to-face.

That evening when she reached home from work, she grabbed the mail from the box and darted into the house, carrying it into the kitchen. The cozy room with its golden oak cabinets and country wallpaper in blue and white print reminded Sally of the kitchen from her childhood when cookies baked in the oven and homemade soup simmered on the stove.

She dropped the mail on the table as the telephone rang. She was greeted by Ed's hearty voice.

"Alice and I plan to see a play at the community theater, and we thought maybe you'd like to join us? We haven't seen much of you lately."

"That's because you only have eyes for each other," she teased. "A play sounds like fun. Thanks for the invitation."

"I'll try for Saturday. Is that okay?"

"Count me in."

Pleased at their thoughtfulness, Sally placed the teakettle on the burner for tea and sat at the table, shuffling through the mail. An unusual postage stamp caught her eye—Africa. A letter from Tim's sister, Beth. Sally tore it open, anxious to hear from her sister-in-law. Beth had been out of the country for a long time doing research for a university. Tim's death had been difficult for her. The two had been very close.

The teakettle whistled, and Sally poured the hot water over a tea bag in her mug. Reading the letter, Sally wondered if she should have encouraged Beth to come home for the funeral. Her trip from Africa would have taken at least a week. At the time, Sally wanted no delay to the horrible nightmare of burial. Beth had listened to her and missed the funeral. Now, Beth's grief was still fresh. First she'd lost her father, then Tim. Now the letter explained her mother, Esther Newgate, was seriously ill.

After Tim's death, Sally felt herself drifting from Tim's mother. The painful memories seemed to be too much for his mom. Though Sally pursued with calls and letters, Esther seemed different. Now Sally wondered if it was her growing illness.

As the tea brewed in the cup, Sally grabbed a table knife from the drawer and slit open the other envelopes. She read the newsy letter from her longtime friend, Elaine Miller. She and her husband, Mark, moved away. Of late, they rarely talked, and she wondered how a thing like that could happen to such close friends. Sometimes, life seemed filled with losses.

four

On the last Tuesday in November the weather turned bitterly cold, and Sally prepared to face her group meeting. She'd been asked to work overtime, but instead brought home a pile of reports to proofread. If seeing Brad hadn't been so important, she would have stayed at the office.

When Sally arrived at Holy Cross Church, she hurried into the foyer, pulling off her woolen scarf and gloves. She glanced around for Brad, but he wasn't there. Finding a seat, she stared at the clock, wondering if he would come at all. Maybe he was too ashamed.

Though she felt apprehensive, she wanted to talk to Brad about the incident Saturday. She prayed the situation had a reasonable explanation. She glanced toward the doorway one last time as Jack stepped to the podium.

Coward, she thought. But suddenly the children came to mind and she worried. Perhaps one of them was ill. She felt distracted, glimpsing around the room again, until she finally gave up, deciding he wasn't coming. A sense of loss showered over her.

Jack's words flowed from the microphone. "Open your heart to those new gifts of friendship, experiences, and love. Allow yourself to heal." His thoughts marched through her head. Brad had stepped into her life, and they had helped each other. But her healing wasn't complete, and she wondered how much time it would take. The utter loneliness was gone. Hope had returned, but she had lost confidence in herself and her judgment.

During the worst times she turned to God, believing He had a plan for her, but lately, she wondered. Even tonight, she realized God had given her a little taste of hope with Brad, then took it away.

When Jack concluded, she rose, and as she headed toward the refreshment table, Brad rushed through the doorway toward her. The expression on his face made her heart skip a beat, whether from fear or joy she wasn't sure.

&

Brad had stood in the doorway watching Sally before she noticed him. When the presentation ended, he hurried to her side. "Sorry I'm late. I wanted to talk to you so badly. Of all things, I had to work overtime. The new designs have to be ready by the end of the month, and you know what that means for the engineering department." He was rattling, and he sensed her coolness.

"I thought maybe one of the kids was sick."

Her tone sounded icy. "No, just work." He hesitated, glancing around the room. "Could we talk privately? I thought maybe we could go for coffee after the meeting. I told the baby-sitter I might be a little later than usual."

"Sorry, I can't. I brought home a ton of work so I didn't have to stay in the office tonight. I didn't want to miss the meeting."

Disappointment washed over him. Was she avoiding him? He didn't blame her if she was. "I've got to talk to you. I need to explain."

She didn't respond, but glanced around the room.

People were already gathering into the small group sessions.

He felt desperate. "Could we at least find a quiet spot in the hall. Anything?" He stepped toward the doorway.

Relief filled him when she followed. He led her to the hall and the door of a small, unoccupied room stood open. They entered. Before they sat, he blurted, "I wanted to explain about Saturday. I was really happy to see you at the party. But I hadn't considered what you might think. . .until it was too late. I was in a spot." The words tumbled from his mouth.

"Yes, we were both uncomfortable."

"You thought I'd lied to you." Her face reflected her feelings. "And I couldn't explain. I'm breaking a promise now talking to you, but our friendship is more important. Darlene's my cousin."

"Your cousin?" She looked at him quizzically.

"She's separated and was uncomfortable going to the party alone. We both know how that feels."

She balked. "She really is your cousin?" Embarrassment swept across her face. "Brad, I'm sorry. I thought—"

"I can imagine. You opened up to me, and you must have thought I was playing games with you, sort of like—"

"Like Steve. Yes. That's what I thought. I was so hurt. Not so much you were with Darlene. . .but you'd deceived me."

She hesitated. She was hurt? Had she been jealous?

"I know. And I'd promised Darlene I wouldn't tell a soul. She'd be so embarrassed if people knew she went to the party with her cousin."

Sally took a finger and crossed her heart. "Promise I won't tell, Brad. I'll keep the secret forever." A deep breath quivered through her. "I feel like a fool."

Brad looked toward the door. He longed to ask her about Ron, but he didn't want to push his luck. Instead, he took her hand, giving it a squeeze. "Friends?"

Her smile overwhelmed him. "Friends," she said.

They returned quickly to the large room where the small group sessions were beginning. Tonight they remained quieter than most evenings. For the first time since he attended the sessions, he felt no need to speak. Talking to Sally and looking into her understanding eyes, seemed all he needed. When the session ended, Brad drew to her side and whispered in her ear. "I wish you could go for coffee."

Her face revealed her disappointment. "Some other time."

Sally's positive response was all he needed. "Great."

Helping her with her coat, they walked to the parking lot together, huddled against the powerful wind whipping everything in its path.

❧

Saturday evening, Ed and Alice picked up Sally for the play at the community theater, and they arrived with only enough time to be ushered hastily to their seats. With sides aching from laughter, the final curtain lowered and they edged into the narrow aisle. As Ed went ahead to get their coats, Sally faltered, hearing a familiar voice.

"Well, well, look who's here."

She gazed wide-eyed into Brad's bright smile. She flushed, being caught off guard. "Well, hello." Pleasure galloped through her, but in a pulse beat, she filled with apprehension and eyed the lobby.

Brad answered her question as she searched the crowd. "I'm here with my friend, Larry, over there." He pointed to a man across the lobby. "He and his wife have season tickets, but she had other plans, so I'm his date."

To her embarrassment, Sally let out an audible sigh of relief. Her face reddened, again. But he didn't seem to notice. She blurted, "I'm here with friends, too."

He looked pleased. "Larry and I drove separately. So, maybe you and your friends would like to go for some dessert and coffee."

Sally's heart fluttered. Tonight, she had no reason to say no, and she responded eagerly. "I'd love to, but let's check with them."

She eyed the crowd, searching for Alice and Ed, and in the lull, she calmed her giddy feelings.

She saw them by the coat check. Sally's coat lay over Ed's arm. With Brad in tow, she hurried to their sides. "Brad, I'd like you to meet my friends, Alice Brown and Ed Washburn. You've heard me mention them in group discussion, I'm sure. They've been my guardian angels, like a mom and dad to me." She turned to Ed and Alice. "This is Brad Mathews."

Ed and Alice beamed at Sally's introduction. "It's so nice to meet you," Alice said with her soft drawl, thrusting her hand forward. Her ladylike manner reminded Sally of a grand Southern lady, like Melanie Wilkes from *Gone With the Wind*.

Brad spoke without hesitation. "It's nice to meet you. I asked Sally if you'd care to join me for some dessert?"

Ed glanced at Alice, and then his gaze rested on Sally's face. "No, I think not, but thanks for asking." Gesturing to Alice, he continued, "I need to get this young lady home before her driver falls asleep at the wheel, but why don't you young people go and enjoy yourselves?"

Sally wanted to hug him. "You're sure you don't mind?" The sentence caused her to grin. "But I suppose you two really don't need a chaperone, do you?"

Ed glanced at Alice. "*We* don't." He squeezed Sally's elbow as he helped her with her coat. They walked together to the parking lot, each couple heading in their own direction.

ॐ

Not far from the theater, Brad spotted a cozy little storefront restaurant still open. A sign in the window advertised Home-made Pies.

They ordered and the pastry, they agreed, did taste home made.

"I told you I was hungry," Brad said, shoveling a forkful

of the nutmeg-scented apple pie and vanilla ice cream into his mouth.

"I noticed," Sally teased.

They dug into their tasty desserts and washed them down with the steaming coffee. Brad's mind spun, trying to decide how to broach the subject of Ron. He set his coffee cup on the table, the words tugging at his heart. "The other night we talked about Darlene, but I'll be honest, I saw you leave the party with the fellow you were talking to, and I wondered about that myself."

Sally's surprised eyes raised from her forkful of raspberry pie. "What do you mean?"

"I noticed you were with him all evening. You said you were alone." He hoped he didn't sound like a pitiful wimp.

Her eyes widened. "You're right. I suppose you wondered like I did." She tilted her head, looking sheepish. "Ron's just Darby's friend. I'd seen him before a couple of times."

Brad's stomach tumbled, and the pie sat like a brick. "But he left the party with you." His mind swirled out a million unwanted pictures. He waited for the bomb.

"He did?" Her brow furrowed. "You're right. He walked me to my car. I had parked down the block, and I suppose he was being a gentleman. That's it. I thought he went back inside. Didn't he?"

Brad felt embarrassed for his suspicions. "No. I'm sure I would have noticed."

She shrugged. "He must have decided to leave. He tried to put me at ease all evening, knowing it was my first party alone."

Brad wanted to kick himself. Naturally, she was uneasy being alone, and then to have him walk in with a date. He sighed. "I'm sorry, Sally. I hadn't thought about that. I suppose the evening was strange for you."

She shook her head. "It was."

"I wish you'd asked me to go. I would've gone with you like I did with Darlene." He shriveled. *That wasn't what I meant to say.* "I mean, I would have *enjoyed* going with you."

She raised her eyes to meet his, a faint grin turning the corners of her mouth. "Thanks. I wish I had asked you."

He gazed at her, tongue-tied. After a lengthy silence, he recovered. "The kids seem to be doing better. Not perfect, but really improved."

"You're blessed to have two nice children." She paused as if struggling with herself. "Lately, I've been sorry we never had a baby. If we had a child, I'd feel like a family. Someone to lavish my love on." She stopped, looking away. "But I see the problems you've had. Then I wonder."

"It's hard, but they're a blessing." He studied her face and unanswered questions stalked through his thoughts. He pushed his fork around on the plate in silence. Then he lifted his eyes to hers. "Didn't you want children?"

Her head jerked upward. "Oh, yes. We both wanted a child." She glanced away. "I had a miscarriage. I felt guilty— as if there was something wrong with me that I couldn't carry the baby to term."

"I'm sorry." His response seemed feeble, in relationship to the sadness on her face.

"It's odd how things work. We were going to try again, but Tim was killed. . . Well anyway, the doctor said I had nothing physically wrong. Miscarriages happen sometimes."

Brad reached across the table and lay his hand on hers. The sensation rocked him. He yearned to hold her against his chest. "I've always believed that God has reasons for everything. We don't always understand though."

"So many things we don't understand." Sally paused. "I

don't know what's gotten into me, telling you all this stuff. Anyway, I suppose we should talk about something more cheerful."

He wanted to tell her how much her words meant to him, to know she liked kids and wanted them in her life. Instead, he opened his heart, and told her about Janet's illness and death, the grief for himself and his children.

She listened, and his sorrow reflected in her eyes. She raised her hand to wipe a tear from her eye. Their past swept before them, and Brad emptied his bottled emotions into a river of hope. His hand still lay on hers. Her warmth helped him feel alive again.

"I'm glad you told me about Janet. It helps to talk about things, doesn't it?"

"Sure does." He could bear no more and took the opportunity to change the subject. "Tell me about the couple you were with tonight."

Sally chuckled. "They're wonderful. I played cupid. I introduced them. Alice goes to my church and really helped me after Tim died. I felt so alone and she offered to sit with me in church to keep me company."

Brad listened, her animation raising his spirits.

"Ed lives down the block," she continued. "He was always a good neighbor. If we needed anything, he was there. He gave Tim a lot of gardening tips. Ed's a wonderful gardener, and he's helped me so much. You should see my garden in the spring."

"I'd love to." Brad's candid comment amazed him.

Sally flushed. "Are you saying you'd like an invitation in the spring?"

"Or sooner." Her smile delighted him. "Maybe you could teach me something about flowers. Janet was the gardener. I tried to keep things growing, but I don't know beans about flowers." They snickered at his picturesque phrase.

From that point, they talked easily, telling each other about their childhoods, their hopes, their dreams, and, after more refills of coffee than Brad could remember, he drove her home, delighted that the evening had moved their relationship a step beyond friendship.

five

On Thursday evening Bill telephoned. "Listen, Sis. Could you do us a big favor?"

"Sure, as long as it's not a loan," she teased.

"No, this is worse than a loan. It's a really big favor. I have to go up to Grand Rapids on Saturday for a business meeting. Sue and I thought we could make it a little trip for us, too, and stay overnight, but we have one small problem."

"Is the small problem a size six?"

"Exactly." Bill chuckled. "We could take her along, but having a night on the town, a romantic dinner, well. . ."

"Say no more. Carrie and I'll get along fine."

"Thanks so much, if you're sure you don't mind."

"What are sisters for?" Ways to entertain Carrie marched through her mind. "Does she have ice skates?"

"Sure does."

"Bring them along."

"She'll be thrilled. The neighbor girl takes her on a little pond, but she spends a lot of time sitting, not skating."

"Don't laugh! I'll probably do the same, and I have much farther to reach the ice than Carrie."

Bill's hearty laugh echoed through the phone.

"Let's not mention the skates, in case I chicken out."

"No problem. I'll bring her by early on Saturday."

"Bring her on Friday night. That'll make it easier." *Easier for you,* she thought as she hung up the receiver. She rolled her eyes. Even if she found her skates, she wasn't sure she could stand on them.

On Friday night, Carrie arrived, and Bill slipped Sally the ice skates, hidden in a large paper bag. The evening was filled with baking chocolate chip cookies and storybooks. Finally, at bedtime, Sally listened to Carrie's prayers, and then pulled the blanket around her shoulders. Kissing her check, she left the door ajar with a relieved sigh.

By the next morning, a light dusting of snow had fallen. The sun was bright, glinting on the white powdery flakes. After breakfast, three puzzles, and two more storybooks, Sally surprised Carrie with the day's plan.

"Ice skating," Carrie moaned, "but I didn't bring my skates."

"Sure you did." Sally displayed the paper bag holding her shiny skates. "Your daddy brought them."

Carrie squealed and clapped her hands.

Sally grabbed the heavy wool sweater from her room and bundled Carrie into her ski pants, sweater, and jacket. With scarves, knit caps, mittens, and ice skates in tow, they hurried out into the bright, crisp morning.

The dusting of snow had begun to melt with the morning sunshine before they arrived at the recreation center. Families glided along the mirrorlike surface of the outdoor rink.

Sally walked, and Carrie flew to a bench near the ice edge. She dropped her skates on the bench and pulled off her boots before Sally could catch her.

"Hold on there, eager beaver. Don't get your feet cold and wet before I can help you." Sally sat beside her on the bench and retrieved her boots from the snow. With speed, she pushed Carrie's feet into her skates, lacing them tightly. Finally Sally laced her own.

"Okay now, are you ready to help your old aunty to the ice?"

"Are you old, Aunt Sally?" A quizzical look crept across her face.

"Just a little bit. Nothing to worry about. Are you ready?"

Sally's question was foolish, for Carrie tugged her toward the ice rink.

Hand in hand, they edged onto the ice, gliding cautiously. When they gained courage, they joined the others circling the smooth, steely ice. Before long they skated together, moving in rhythm.

Sally's courage overtook her wisdom as she pivoted to face Carrie. Instead, she and Carrie found themselves sprawled on the ice in a heap. They sat on the cold surface and laughed, embarrassed, but unharmed. Sally, trying to stand, tripped herself again. Suddenly two arms reached down, grabbed her by the waist, and helped her rise.

"Is this a new skating technique? I've seen the double axel, but this is a new one."

Her heart leaped as she looked into Brad's glinting eyes, his cheeks glowing from the cold. A knitted half-cap covered his ears, and a lock of hair curled on his forehead.

"Brad, I didn't know you were coming here." She clamped her mouth closed, hearing her exuberance bubbling without control.

"I'm glad I did. You can meet the kids." He turned and waved at two young skaters, carefully heading his way.

"Kelly, Danny, I want you to meet Sally Newgate. She's in the group I go to." The two children looked up at Sally, shyly. "Can you say hello?" Brad urged.

"Uh-huh." Danny nodded, but Kelly only looked at her and then at Carrie.

"Well," Sally said, "I'm glad to meet you. Your daddy talks about you all the time. This is my niece, Carrie. Her mom and dad are out of town."

Brad leaned down, resting his hand on Carrie's shoulder. "Hi, Carrie. Your aunt has told me about you, too."

"Did she tell you that we made cookies last night?" Carrie

asked. "They're chocolate chip."

"No. She didn't. I imagine they're delicious. Kelly loves baking cookies, too." He glimpsed at his daughter, but she remained silent. Brad looked at Sally with frustration. He darted to a new subject. "Been here long?"

"About an hour. It's a perfect day. I wasn't sure if I'd remember how to skate. And I wasn't doing too badly. . . until I fell."

He grinned. "The kids are just learning, so we try to get here at least once on the weekend."

"Daddy, let's go and skate." Kelly pulled at his jacket, urging her father toward the skaters. "Come on," she insisted.

"Kelly, in a minute. I'm talking. Skate with Danny."

She folded her arms across her chest. "I don't want to skate with Danny. I want to skate with you." Her young face puckered in anger. Danny waited, silently.

Brad's shoulders drooped. "Please, don't be rude." He gestured them forward. "Let's all skate together." He dug his skate in the ice and glided along next to Sally. Carrie joined Danny and Kelly.

But Kelly stopped, facing her father. "I don't want to skate with other people. I want to skate with you."

Brad's expression shifted between defeat and embarrassment. "I'm sorry, Sally. She's usually not a rude kid."

"I'm not a kid. I'm seven." Kelly's young voice became strident, and she looked ready to cry. Brad stared in confusion.

"Brad, we're getting ready to take a break. The three of you go ahead, and I'll talk to you later."

Brad offered a grateful nod. Sally watched as they skated back toward the circling crowd. Sally and Carrie headed for a small refreshment stand where the aroma of coffee and hot chocolate drifted on the air. With a hot chocolate in their hands, they navigated to the benches near the ice rink.

"How come that girl wasn't nice?" Carrie asked.

"Well, she's confused, Carrie."

"Was she mad at us? She acted mad at *us*."

"No, I think she's a little jealous of us taking her daddy's attention. Kelly's mommy died, and she needs lots of love and attention right now. So we should forgive her."

"Okay. Let's forgive her." Carrie quickly changed the subject and sipped her hot chocolate. Sally listened to Carrie's chatter only halfheartedly. Her thoughts were preoccupied with Brad and Danny and the very unhappy young girl between them. The last she noticed them, they were heading toward the parking lot.

&

After church on Sunday, Brad scurried off to the bedroom and pulled Sally's phone number from his wallet. He punched in the numbers, looking over his shoulder like an accomplice to a crime.

When the ringing stopped, he heard a young voice say in a very business-like voice, "Newgate residence."

"Hi Carrie, this is Brad. I met you skating yesterday." He heard nothing and figured she was shaking her head. "Would you tell your Aunt Sally I'm on the telephone?"

"Okay." He heard a clink as she placed the telephone down, and she called out, "Auntie Sally, it's for you. It's that skating man." Then in a nearly inaudible breathy whisper, she added, "The one with the rude girl."

He couldn't help but smile.

In a flash, Sally greeted him. "Hi. How did you make out yesterday?"

Brad cringed, remembering. "I'm really sorry. I thought we'd made progress, but I was wrong. After we left, she clammed up, so I just let it go, rather than make it worse."

"Probably for the best. When Carrie and I went for hot

chocolate, a thought crossed my mind." She stopped speaking for a minute, then her voiced lowered. "But now isn't the time."

He imagined Carrie nearby listening to the conversation.

Her volume raised. "I'll tell you when I see you."

"You can see I need help." He glanced over his shoulder again. "I guess I'd better get off the phone before they get suspicious. I let Kelly and Danny make cookies, and I sneaked off to the bedroom to call. Who knows what mess I'll find?"

She chuckled. "Are they chocolate chip, by any means?"

"What else? Kelly talked cookie-baking since she heard Carrie say she had made some. Kids! Don't you love them?"

"Actually, I do." Her voice smiled.

"I know you do." His heart raced, thinking how important her statement was to him. "See you Tuesday."

"Have fun and eat a cookie in my honor."

❧

At their Tuesday meeting, Sally and Brad stood near the back, waiting for the presentation to begin. "So, what did you want to tell me?" Brad asked.

"Well, when I took Carrie to the zoo a few weeks ago, she asked me questions about dying. Carrie and I hadn't talked about Tim's death before. I was shocked when she asked if I wanted to die to be with Tim. It tore me up. She hugged me and said she was afraid that I'd die like Uncle Tim." Sally ached, remembering the day clearly.

Brad's eyes widened. "You think the kids are worried that I might die and leave them like Janet?" Confusion etched his face.

A sigh raked through her. "Something like that. They lost their mother and don't want to lose their father—to death *or* to someone else. Now, it's all the same to them. Kelly wants your full attention. She doesn't want to share you."

"I give the kids extra time, but maybe that's not enough."

"I don't think it has to do with time as much as fear. They need to be assured you won't leave them—in any way."

Brad placed his hands on her shoulders, searching her eyes. "You make it sound simple."

"It's easy when it's someone else's problem. I don't see my own solutions at all. I don't think people ever do."

He dropped his hands, shifting from one foot to the other uncomfortably. "Listen, I wanted to talk to you tonight about something else. I may as well fess up."

Sally held her breath, wondering.

"And promise you won't compare me to that guy at work."

"Hey, you convinced me, it's hard for a man to keep his hands off a wonderful, delightful person like myself." She teased, fluttering her eyelashes. Her pulse raced.

"That's true, but I'll try. My company holds an annual hayride—or sleigh ride if there's snow, and I'd love you to come along." He rested his hand on her shoulder. "And if you agree, I'll be a perfect gentleman. "

Her heart pressed on her vocal chords. She steadied herself, not wanting to sound like an overanxious teenager. "I haven't been on a hayride in years. It sounds like fun. Is it for families?"

"No, adults only. A real date. I'd love you to come."

"When is it?"

"Saturday." He looked sheepish. "I've waited a long time to ask you, but I've felt as nervous as a schoolboy."

She grinned, feeling as nervous as he. "How can I resist?"

As they headed for their seats, her hands trembled so badly she put them in her pocket so he didn't notice.

❧

The night of the hayride fresh white snow covered the ground. Tonight Brad's heart sat on his sleeve and lay on his tongue.

The words and thoughts had skittered around in his mind—
romance, love, commitment—but he hesitated to lay them out
in the open. If Sally rejected him, he couldn't deal with the
hurt—not yet. But the desire to speak his emotions tripped on
his tongue, and he swallowed to hold them at bay.

As couples jumped and hoisted themselves to the wagons,
they found a space and settled in. With a jingle of bells, the
horses shuddered, the wagon lurched, and they were on their
way.

"Warm enough?" Brad asked, hoping for the opportunity
to move closer.

"A little chilly."

"Then, let's move back," he said, scooting back from the
edge of the wagon and onto the hay. She followed, and they
nestled together in the chilled air.

Before they had moved around the bend into the woods,
the first wagon's passengers burst into song, and their group
joined in. Sally's sweet, full voice rang in Brad's ears, and he
wanted to yell to the world that he was falling in love. Soon
the third wagon added their voices. Old campfire songs
echoed through the woods.

Time passed and a light snow drifted down, its presence
glistening in the moonlight. Brad slid his arm around Sally's
shoulder, feeling foolishly shy. "Warm enough? I felt you
tremble."

"I'm fine—cozy. I think it's the bumpy ride."

But Brad looked into her eyes, sparkling in the moonlight
and sensed a different reason. Sally shifted, resting her hand
on the straw next to his, and even through their gloves, he
felt her nearness. He covered her fingers with his, searching
her eyes for approval. She flashed a shy smile in his direction, and he filled with utter joy. Lifting his eyes, he looked
toward heaven, confident that God had sent her to him.

But the peaceful moment ended. Without warning, a wad of hay flew into Sally's hair, and she tossed a handful back. Then, more hay flew past like a school cafeteria food fight.

"Can't get away with that," Brad called, grabbing a handful for himself, and as he threw the wad of straw through the air, the wagon lumbered into a clearing. The lights of the lodge glowed before them, and the wagon lumbered on with a trail of hay dropping to the ground and voices echoing with laughter. Though Brad joined in the merriment, he yearned to keep Sally wrapped in his arms.

❧

When Sally saw the lights of the lodge, she felt a twinge of disappointment. She wished the ride would go on forever. Nestled in Brad's arms, his hand on hers, she experienced feelings that had lain dormant deep within her far too long. She had questioned God about her life and where it was going. Was this what He'd planned for her?

The wagon came to a halt, and immediately snow missiles replaced the hay. Couples scurried from the wagons, skittering through the white glistening drifts, chasing one another with yells and giggles.

Sally snickered to herself as she slid from the wagon, intent on joining the fun. Her heart thudded, as she scooped up a ball of snow. When Brad jumped from the wagon, she drew in a deep breath and barreled him with her cold, white weapon.

She skirted away from his attack and darted past him, heading for the lodge. But he was hot on her trail. As she veered around the wagon, her boots slipped beneath her. She gasped and tried to maintain her balance, but Brad caught up to her, grabbing her in his arms with a handful of snow.

Her heart pounded with the childish fun, and she bolted away, until they both tumbled to the ground, laughter and breath bursting from their chests. Sally lay on her back, defending herself from his white icy weapon, her pulse racing from his nearness. He lifted himself on an elbow, his face inches from hers. Her racing, joyful heart soared, as their laughter died away, and his gaze sought hers with longing.

"If I hadn't guaranteed I'd be a gentleman, you'd be in deep trouble." His voice sounded breathless—from the chase or from their nearness, she didn't know.

At that moment, she wished he hadn't promised. The words "forget the promise" rose to her lips, but she forced herself to make light of the situation. "Should I call you Steve?"

His lips paused an inch from hers. The warmth of his breath brushed her face, and the aroma of sweet, fresh spearmint invaded her senses. Her heartbeat raced in anticipation. Brad hesitated. "No, but you can call me stupid. A promise is a promise." His lips touched her cheek tenderly, and he raised himself from the ground, leaving Sally with a sense of longing.

As he helped Sally rise, she struggled to gain composure. Brad took her hand, and they headed into the lodge. Her cheek tingled where his lips had pressed, and she longed to kiss his full, tender mouth. Yet they'd known each other only a few months. They had time—*a time for every purpose under heaven*. She'd wait for God's guidance.

six

On Thanksgiving Day, Sally attended worship. For once, she could lean back and enjoy the service, not worrying about the oven timer or reviewing the list of tasks to complete when she returned home. This Thanksgiving Sue's parents were visiting from Florida, and Bill and Sue had invited her for dinner. Her only responsibility was to bring coleslaw and a cranberry mold.

After dinner, they sat around the living room, fighting sleep and wishing they had pulled away from the table sooner. Bill stretched out on the floor and propped his head on a pillow. "Okay, Sis, give."

Sally scowled. "Give what?"

"You've been scarce lately. I've called you and so has Sue, and you're never home. Something's happening in your life." He rolled over, eyeing her.

Knowing Bill, he would drift off sound asleep in a few minutes. But the question had been posed. "Overtime, grief group, church, that's about it." She felt uneasy. Bill was too observant and too opinionated. Though a year and a half had passed, Tim's death seemed fresh in everyone's mind. She wondered if he and Sue would understand about Brad.

"Okay, okay. Forget I asked." He rolled over on his back. "I just want to make sure you're not running around. I know you're lonely, but you have to be careful. That's all." Within a minute, his deep breathing announced he had fallen asleep.

Sally forced herself to chat and grin, but inside she felt irritated and guilty. She didn't like Bill's comment. "Running around" sounded terrible. On top of that, she'd avoided the truth. She could hear her mother's words, echoing from their childhood. "Children, one lie leads to another and another. Oh, what a tangled web we weave when first we practice to deceive." She forced her attention back to the conversation. It hadn't been a lie exactly—perhaps more, the sin of omission. But his words stayed in her head. Was their relationship a mistake?

A few days later, Brad called with a favor. He wanted to give Kelly another try and invited Sally to join them for an animated Christmas display at the mall. His voice pleaded, and Sally didn't have the to heart to refuse.

When Sally opened the door, she knew she was in trouble by the expression on Brad's face. "Problems?"

His head nodded slowly. "Sort of. We'll have to work on it. I'm sorry to put you through this again. I hope once we're on our way things will change."

Her heart dropped like a weight against her stomach. "No problem. What are friends for?" Another fib. She saw the spider weaving the webs her mother warned her about.

She zipped her jacket and followed him to the car. Kelly and Danny sat in the back seat. Danny eyed her as she climbed in, leaning forward with curiosity, but Kelly sat, arms folded across her little chest, pressing herself as far in the corner of the seat as she could.

Sally smiled into the backseat. "Hi. This should be fun. Did your daddy tell you where we're going?"

Danny looked with half-lowered eyelids and nodded. "Uh-huh. To see some fairytale people."

"I can't wait." She turned to Kelly. "Are you excited, Kelly?"

Kelly stared out the window, her lips pressed tightly together. Sally thought she would get no response at all, but without looking, Kelly mumbled, "No."

Brad glanced at Sally helplessly. She signaled him not to say anything and turned back facing the front. Maybe if they ignored the problem it would go away.

They drove in silence with only an occasional comment about traffic or some unimportant topic. Sally knew they were both preoccupied with Kelly's behavior and her sadness.

The Summit Place Mall parking lot overflowed. Shoppers—the courageous warriors out to grab up their first Christmas bargains—scurried in and out of stores. Brad found a parking spot and squeezed in with little room to open their doors. Sally eased out, and Danny followed behind her without hesitation. But Brad stood helplessly on the other side of the car, door open wide, with Kelly refusing to leave the backseat. She continued to sit, arms folded and eyes closed.

Brad pleaded. "Kelly, we're all looking forward to the display. I can't let you sit here by yourself. I wouldn't be a good daddy to do that. You'd be cold. Please come along."

She didn't respond.

Sally's heart ached as she watched the scene. Many parents might have dragged her out by her arm, threatening untold punishments. But Brad knelt down by the door and spoke softly to her. An occasional word drifted from the open door, "understand. . .okay. . .love." Finally, Brad rose, pulling back the seat, and Kelly exited the car, still silent, but walking along beside them.

Though Kelly warmed to the animated displays, she kept Sally blocked from her view. Sally pondered what to do. She had little choice but to accept the situation. God had given her a taste of joy, but she felt it sinking into the mire of despair.

When they stepped outside to the mall parking lot, the snow blew horizontally from the force of the wind, and Brad struggled to clean his windshield. Snow mounded against anything stationary. With effort, he pulled out of the lot.

Salt trucks rumbled in front of them on the road, and the snow plows headed in every direction across the city. Brad drove slowly, finally arriving at Sally's door.

❧

Brad gazed at Sally, knowing he had to talk to her privately for at least a moment. With his eye on the children, he walked her to the door, stepping into the foyer for a moment.

"I'm sorry again, Sally. What can I say? I'd really hoped today would be better." Frustration tore through him. "I know it takes time, and I have to be patient."

Sally rested her hand on his arm. "One of these days, she'll understand that someday you're going to fall in love. But first, she has to know that you still love her."

Her words gave him hope, but part of the comment troubled him. *Someday you'll fall in love.* Didn't she sense that he had tremendous feelings for her? Each time they parted he wanted to cling to her.

So many people he'd spoken with about Sally treated his feelings like puppy love. He recalled some of Darlene's comments. Everyone reminded him they had only met a few months earlier. They reminded him Sally was the first woman he'd been out with since Janet.

Everyone made jokes about hormones and urges. Yes, he was human. He wanted to hold a woman again, to feel her body next to his, but the woman in his thoughts had a face. A lovely face. Sally's. But his feelings were far more than hormones.

Brad squelched the desire to talk with Sally about his feelings. He needed time to understand things himself. His hormones and urges might cry out for release, but an outlet for passion wasn't the reason for his attraction. Brad felt sure, positive, that she was the one to make his life whole and complete again.

Sally gazed at him. "You'd better go. The kids are waiting, and the snow's getting worse." She lay her hand on his arm.

Brad covered it with his own. "If the snow's too deep tomorrow, don't try to clear it yourself. If I can get out, I'll come over and help you."

"Don't worry about me. You get home." She tilted her head with a grin. "But would you call me? So I know you're okay."

"I sure will." He was touched by her worry. When she closed the door, he wished he had acted on his instinct. He longed to slip deeper inside the house, away from the children's eyes, and kiss her good night. Instead, he settled for her wave from the doorway and headed home, feeling lonely.

☙

The city officials declared a snow emergency that evening, and the next morning schools and businesses were closed for the day, including Davidson Electric. Sally stared outside, seeing the huge drifts of snow against the garage door and knew she was housebound unless she attacked the white prison.

With relief, Sally found the shovel on the back porch. And as always, Ed came up the drive with his snowblower. He worked on the heavy white mounds while she shoveled at the garage door. Before he finished the driveway, Ed turned off the machine to give Sally a hand, and in the lull, she heard the telephone ring. She slipped and slid back to the house.

"Hello," she said, panting to catch her breath.

"How are you doing?"

She beamed hearing Brad's voice. "Pretty good. I tackled a snowdrift against the garage door, and Ed showed up with his snowblower to clear the driveway. We're nearly done."

"I hoped to get over, but it took me forever to dig my car out. The kids are having a wonderful time. You should see the snow angel and snowmen. . ." He paused. "Anyway, I have to run a couple of errands. And while I'm out, what if I pick you up and bring you here for dinner?"

Sally heard apprehension in his voice. One thing about Brad, he never gave up.

"Maybe if Kelly gets to know you, she'll perk up a little bit. You can see what an optimistic fellow I am."

"I like optimism, but don't get your hopes up. Still, I'd love to come to dinner."

"Great, I'll be there around five."

"I'll be waiting." She felt as if she'd burst. How could her heartstrings tangle so quickly around his? In wonder, Sally returned to the yard to retrieve the shovel from Ed and finish clearing the snow.

When Brad arrived, Sally saw him through the window. He tooted the horn and stepped from the car, encouraging Kelly to move to the backseat where Danny already sat. Kelly slumped further down in the front seat, shaking her head no.

Sally eyed Kelly as she approached the car and smiled. "How about if I ride in the backseat with Danny?"

Brad looked at her, gratefulness reflecting on his face. Kelly sidled a glance at Sally. A glimmer of thanks shone for a moment, but was quickly covered.

Sally greeted the children and climbed into the back, fastening her seat belt. "Well, Danny, your daddy tells me you made a wonderful snowman in the backyard."

"Uh-huh. We made two, one for me and one for Kelly."

Kelly inched back against her seat, her ear tilted toward them, straining to hear their conversation over the noise of the automobile.

Sally grinned to herself. "Did you give your snowman a top hat like Frosty?"

"Nope, but one snowman has on Daddy's cap, and they both have scarves." Before Sally could speak, he changed subjects. "Did Daddy tell you I helped Kelly bake cookies?"

"Yep. I hope I can try one."

"Sure. You can have two."

"Thank you. You're very generous." Pleasure filled her. Danny's usual shyness seemed to have vanished.

The ride to Brad's house was short. The attractive homes in the small village of Huntington Woods had been built of dark red brick with gray slate roofs, and thick ivy, clinging to the chimneys, added charm. Beveled glass windows glinted from stairwells and doorways.

Brad pulled into the driveway, and the door rose, giving them access to the large attached garage. In the back hall, they hung their coats on hooks in the hallway, and the children placed their boots on a boot tray next to the back door, impressing Sally by their neatness.

Her first view was the cozy kitchen with rich cherry cabinets and a butcher block island. "This is lovely, Brad." Janet's feminine touches were everywhere.

She passed through the dining room, decorated with a small floral beige and raspberry print wallpaper extending from the cove ceiling to the chair railings. Below the chair railing, the wall was painted in rich raspberry. A long fruitwood table stood in the center, and a china cabinet filled with lovely old dishes covered one wall.

Sally gazed into the cabinet. "You collect antiques."

"Janet did, but I like them."

The living room impressed her with a floor-to-ceiling French pane bay window looking out on a sprawling backyard now covered with snow and guarded by two winter-garbed snowmen.

The room stretched from the front of the house to the back. A stone fireplace on a side wall formed a conversation area around the stone hearth. She could picture Brad and a faceless woman sitting there on cold winter nights, and she felt a twinge of melancholy.

"Beautiful, Brad. And a wonderful setting."

"Thanks."

He opened his mouth as if to say more, but Danny returned with a selection of storybooks and headed directly toward Sally.

She gave Brad a secret smile as Danny scampered beside her on the love seat. "Well, Danny, what kind of books do you have there?"

He offered her the stack of books.

She skimmed over the titles. "Let me see, *The Little Engine That Could, The Wooden Soldier,* and here's one about you, *Danny Goes for a Ride.*" She held the book toward him.

Danny nodded his head.

"Would you like me to read you this one?"

"Yep," he said, and they began.

ੴ

Brad occupied himself building a fire in the fireplace. He watched Sally nestled on the cushions with Danny, and his thoughts drifted to Janet. A wave of sorrow washed through him, not only for himself, but for the children. Sally's presence in the house brought back a surge of memories.

Kelly returned from her room and sat with her eyes focused on Sally. Brad knew, from Sally's occasional glance, she hoped Kelly would join them. "Do you like to read stories, Kelly?"

She sat at a distance, swinging her legs. "Yes, but my books are more grown-up." Her eyes stayed riveted on Sally. Brad's heart ached for his child.

"That's because you're older," Sally said. "You're seven, aren't you?"

Brad watched the interaction with awe.

"Uh-huh. I was seven in October."

Danny chimed in. "My birthday's in July. I'll be six."

Brad hid his grin, watching them vie for attention.

"Then, I can go to school for a whole day."

"That's great," Sally said. "You'll learn to read by yourself, and you'll be nearly as grown-up as Kelly."

Brad eyed Kelly, and she beamed when Sally called her "grown-up." Brad marveled at Sally's way with the children.

"Then I won't have to do everything for you, Danny," Kelly said, rising from her chair and wandering to the arm of the love seat nearest Sally. "You'll be able to do things all by yourself."

Brad felt a weight lift from his shoulders. Sally would make a wonderful mother. But Janet loomed again in his thoughts. He imagined Sally living in this house, changing things, and he wondered if he'd ever be free of the guilt that hung in his thoughts.

Though he needed to prepare dinner, Brad longed to stay and watch the children with Sally. Before he tore himself away, Kelly asked if they could watch television. With the young ones in front of the TV, he invited Sally to join him in the kitchen.

She stood next to him at the counter and breathed a sigh. "I think I made some progress, but I'm exhausted."

"I couldn't keep my eyes off of you. You're wonderful. You handled Kelly so well." He patted her back lightly, fighting himself from taking her in his arms.

She poked his ribs, and he flinched.

She wrinkled her nose. "Didn't think I could do it, huh? To be honest, neither did I. I amazed myself."

They talked while Brad worked on the steaks. Sally cleaned the green beans, putting them in a steamer. While Brad set the table, Sally volunteered to make the salad and busied herself with washing and slicing the vegetables.

With the food ready, they sat around the table and bowed their heads. Brad thanked God for their blessings as emotions tugged at his heart. Through half-closed eyes, he caught the image of Sally in Janet's seat at the table. His heart lurched, and he swallowed to hold back the tremor that moved through his body. They joined in the "Amen," and Brad added a silent postscript to God, asking for guidance.

"This is great," Sally said, running the knife through the tender steak. "You're a gourmet."

"What's a gourmet?" Danny asked. "Are you one, Daddy?"

Brad set his face with a serious expression. "If Sally says I am, then I guess I am."

Danny looked quizzical.

"A gourmet is a very good cook—like in a wonderful restaurant," Sally explained.

"My daddy is a gourmet," Kelly agreed.

Brad and Sally controlled their laughter.

"Well, then I guess that's that," Brad concluded.

Kelly was in charge of dessert. She brought out ice cream and proudly displayed a plate of her homemade cookies, that Sally duly complimented.

Brad walked in a dream through the evening, thrilled, grateful, and confused. The emotions that sneaked into his consciousness bothered him. New fears and questions arose, but he tucked them away, praying time would smooth them into nothing.

Before the children's bedtime arrived, Brad arranged for the neighbor girl to sit with the children while he drove Sally home. They finished a final game of Candyland, and Brad tucked the children into bed and listened to their prayers. When Katie arrived, Brad and Sally headed for the car and the ride home.

In her driveway, Sally lingered for a moment. "It was a wonderful evening, Brad. Thanks for inviting me. Your home is lovely, and you really are a gourmet."

"Thanks." He shifted in the seat to face her. "Seriously, Sally, I enjoyed having you there. I was proud of Kelly. She seemed more like herself. You did a great job with her."

"They're wonderful, Brad. When I sat with Danny reading the storybook, I realized how much they must miss their mom."

Words hung on his lips. He wanted to release the thoughts that hammered in this head, but he couldn't say it all, not yet, not until he understood it himself. "Some of the same thoughts went through my mind."

"Maybe it was good for them to have a woman in the house."

Brad placed his hand on her cheek, and his eyes searched hers. Did Sally understand how he felt? Did she sense his own needs? "It was good for them and for me. You're the first woman in our home since Janet—a woman who isn't family, I mean. It seemed. . .strange. But nice." He felt the longing move through him, not for Janet, but for Sally. He caressed her cheek, then his fingers nestled in her chestnut curls. She shuddered, and he returned his hand to her cool, soft skin. He wanted her to be his at that moment, but instead, he leaned forward, placing his lips on her cheek where his hand had been. "I can't say in words what this evening has meant to me."

Her gaze sought his. She placed her hand over his. "Next time, it's my treat."

Her words lay on his ear. Before he responded, she squeezed

his hand and opened the car door. He couldn't let her go like this. He touched her arm, urging her back. Leaning forward, he pressed his lips tentatively to hers, then drew away.

She pressed her fingers against her lips, her eyes scarching his. Then she slid from the car and hurried to the porch. She waved from her foyer, and he backed out of the driveway, heading home to the children with anxious thoughts careening like bumper cars through his mind.

ॐ

The next morning Sally awoke with the previous evening's memories swirling in her head. The kiss happened so gently and with such haste she had wondered if it were only wishful thinking, but when she looked in a mirror, she knew it had been real. The emotion overwhelmed her. She recalled Ed's words. *It will happen. You'll feel it for sure.*

Her feelings for Brad were growing rapidly—too rapidly, perhaps. Apprehension rose in her. Sitting in his home, she had felt Janet's presence. She tried to block the thoughts from her mind, but they lingered throughout the evening. Could she risk being hurt again?

Janet had been gone for a little more than a year. Was that enough time for Brad to know his heart? He cared for her. She saw his struggle as she felt her own—the passion, the longing. Time was the answer. They needed to move slowly. But saying the words didn't stop the race pounding through her heart.

seven

The days flew by. Sally approached the holidays as joyful as the colored lights and the decorated buildings. She and Brad grew closer each day, and for Sally, Christmas this year promised to be special. Yet amid the joy and thrill of their blossoming relationship, fears nudged her. Kelly was yet far from total acceptance of her, and Sally had yet to tell Bill and Sue about Brad. Their comments at Thanksgiving left a tainted memory in her mind. Yet keeping him a secret put a damper on her happiness.

The grief sessions were drawing to a close. This evening, everyone gathered around the large hall filled with holiday spirit.

Following Jack's presentation, Brad took her arm and whispered in her ear, "Who knew coming to these meetings would be so important? I met you."

Sally avoided looking into his eyes for a moment. She fought back the tears that edged their way into hers. Some people couldn't express their feelings, and Brad sharing his with her meant nearly as much as the words he said.

"I feel the same, Brad." Sally struggled to contain her emotions. "I think about *you* now, instead of feeling sorry for myself."

He put his arm around her, pulling her close, and she flushed, realizing that others were watching them.

Instead of the small group sessions, they celebrated Christmas with an elaborate spread of snacks and desserts. Later, one of the facilitators played the piano, and everyone gathered around and sang carols.

Brad and Sally mingled with the others. She beamed at Brad as she listened to his excellent baritone voice resounding, "Oh, come let us adore Him, Christ the Lord." When the party neared an end, the pianist concluded with "Silent Night." Brad took her hand in his, and her eyes misted as they stood together, singing her favorite carol.

When Brad pulled into her driveway, he nuzzled her in his arms and drew her to him. His warm, tender lips touched hers and lingered, filling her with a sweet sense of completeness. He leaned back, searching her eyes. "I've wanted to kiss you like this for a long time."

"And I've wanted you to."

Embracing her, he kissed her hair and her forehead. His body trembled as did her own, and their lips met again, softly, yet completely. "You are so beautiful," he said.

Tears slid from her eyes. She had not heard those words since Tim said them to her so long ago.

❧

Sally sat at the computer, a pile of accounts in front of her. The approaching holiday also meant the year-end inventory. She squinted at the screen, her eyes aching, and a headache edged its way up the cords of her neck. She wondered if she were catching a cold. Glancing at her wristwatch, she hoped the hand was nearing five o'clock, but the hour hand rested only a hair past the three.

She massaged her shoulders and ran her fingers along the tension below her hairline. She lowered her hands and refocused on the numbers spread across the computer screen. Without warning, warm fingers kneaded the tension in her neck, and she spun on her chair in surprise. She gasped when her eyes focused on Steve, a slack grin formed on his lips.

"What are you doing?" Sally drew back from his hands suspended before her.

"Helping you relax. I saw you rub your neck. It's much more enjoyable when someone else massages those tender spots."

"I don't think so." Her words swung at him like a whip.

He backed away from her angry words. His hands flexed defensively, as if to hold back her verbal daggers. "Sorry. I thought I was doing a good deed. You looked like you could use a little relaxation."

She wished she could erase the moment and start again. Anger solved nothing. "Look, Steve, I'm sorry I snapped, but you surprised me. Please, don't do me any more favors. Okay?"

Her kindness, apparently, came across as encouragement. Steve seated himself on the corner of her desk with a wink. "Okay. You're right. Next time, I'll ask permission first."

"There won't be a next time." She slid her papers closer to the computer and faced the screen. He didn't move and watched her. She pivoted her chair a fraction in his direction. "Did you want something?"

His grin broadened into a leering smile. "You don't have to ask, do you?"

She shuddered. "If you have nothing serious to say, I'd like you to leave. I'm in the middle of inventory, and I need to concentrate."

He rose from the desk as if in slow motion, and as he passed her chair, his finger traced the line of her arm. Sally closed her eyes and remained still. Any word and she would only encourage him. He didn't seem to understand what she said. Yet at the moment, she had no desire to explain herself to him. Maybe Darby could give her a tip about discouraging unwanted attention. She didn't seem to have the knack. Not one iota.

ঝ

Two weeks before Christmas, Brad paced in his living room, knowing he had to call with news that would dampen Sally's spirit. He wanted to phrase it right, to let her know he was disappointed, too. When he had his words in order, he trudged to the telephone. "I dreamed of us spending some of the holiday together, but I've had an unexpected change in plans."

"What is it, Brad?"

He heard anxiety in her voice. "My mother convinced us to fly to the Cape for the holidays. I hope you're not too disappointed."

"Why? What happened? I thought you said she was coming here."

This time he heard disappointment. "She was under the weather for a couple of weeks and said she doesn't feel up to traveling during the Christmas rush. I'm really sorry—and disappointed."

"I was looking forward to the holiday, but I know your mother must love having you all there." Despite her bravado, he could envision her downcast eyes.

Brad felt torn by her disappointment. "She loves having us there, but I think she's disappointed, too. She hoped to meet you."

Her voice softened. "I'm sorry to sound like a baby. I'm disappointed. Will you spend the whole holiday there? Maybe you could come home between Christmas and New Year. We could still have some time together. How about New Year's Eve?"

Desperation coursed through him. Would she understand what he had to tell her? "I'm sorry, Sally. When I agreed to go to the Cape, Mother planned a full agenda, and I've already made arrangements."

"Oh, and they can't be changed?" Her voice dwindled to a murmur.

"I had a difficult time getting airplane tickets so I added vacation days to the regular Christmas holiday. We're leaving earlier and returning later than most travelers. It worked out best that way."

"Oh."

Her utter disappoint ricocheted in his thoughts. "I'm sorry."

A sigh rattled from her. "I guess I understand."

❧

When they disconnected, Sally felt ashamed. Normally, she behaved better. But today, her emotions wavered between anger and disappointment. Tears rolled down her cheeks. She was being selfish. If her mother were alive, Sally would visit her for the holiday without a second thought—especially if she'd been ill.

Her disappointment doubled as she thought it through. He'd be gone, but most of all, he hadn't asked her to come with him. She shook her head. She knew the answer. Their relationship was too new. Asking her to join him wasn't appropriate. Though she said the words, the hurt and disappointment stayed.

Sally struggled with the situation, sorting it out in her mind. A new romance offered both ups and downs. She opened up and felt the joy of being wanted again. But giving her heart to Brad made her vulnerable. Her own emotions hung by a string. Sally feared losing him. She wanted to keep him in her sight, to guard him. Now, she'd acted like a thoughtless child.

Sally dug deep to locate her compassion. Christmas would be difficult for Kelly and Danny. Being with their grandmother would ease their sadness. What would ease her sadness?

Distraction was what she needed, something to get rid of her disappointment. She delved into her work at Davidson's, and the final preparations for Christmas. Then on Sunday after church, she walked through her back door to the ringing of the telephone. Without taking off her coat, she grabbed the receiver.

"Hi, Sally, this is Ron."

"Ron." Her heart skipped a beat, and she flushed with discomfort. She hadn't spoken to him since Darby's birthday party. "It's been a long time."

"Sorry I haven't called you sooner, but I've been working long hours on a new training program. I'm thankful it's about over." He paused. "But I've thought about you a lot."

Sally hadn't thought about him at all. "Things are happening around here, too." Brad had happened—that was more truthful. Then, she tensed, wondering why he'd called.

"Eric asked me to make some calls for him. He's planning a surprise for Darby next weekend. It's one of his brainstorm ideas, so it's short notice. He thought you'd like to be there."

"Surprise?" Her curiosity was piqued.

"Yep—a surprise party."

"It's not her birthday. We just celebrated that."

"No, it's not her birthday—but I'm sworn to secrecy. He's having a small dinner party on Saturday. Can you come?"

She hesitated. Was he asking her for a date or only telling her about the party?

"I'll pick you up. Eric has a private dining room at Aunt Fanny's. . .on Woodward."

Picking her up? But what was the occasion? "Come on, Ron. Give me a hint. I wouldn't miss a special party for Darby, but. . ." Sally thought for a moment, and then the party's purpose dawned on her. "Ron, are they engaged? He's going to propose to her, isn't he? It has to be that! Am I right?"

"I never told you a thing, Sally," he chuckled.

The excitement prickled up her arms. "I wouldn't miss it for the world. But I'm just around the corner from Aunt Fanny's. I'll drive there myself. Thanks anyway."

"It's no problem, Sally. Why take two cars?"

She felt foolish arguing with him, and she didn't want to tell him about Brad on the telephone. In person seemed better. Yet, guilt marched through her. Would Brad's mother plan a date for him in her plethora of scheduled activities? Jealousy inched into her thoughts, and she shuddered. "What time, Ron?"

"How's seven? And don't say a word, I'll pick you up."

She bit her lip, wondering how she would keep the excitement out of her face when she talked to Darby.

❧

Brad looked into the embers of Sally's fireplace and then returned to her eyes. Her disappointment clung in his thoughts. If the situation were reversed, he'd feel the same way.

She stared toward the sparking fire. "I need to apologize to you. I behaved like a pouty, pleading child. I hope you forgive me. I know it's important for the kids to be with family. I'm sorry I sounded so pitiful."

Her chestnut hair glinted red highlights in the glow of the flames. "If you didn't care about me, you wouldn't have cared. How's that for a sentence?" He grinned and rose from the chair, crossing to the love seat.

He sat beside her and slipped his arm around her shoulder, nestling her head under his chin. She lay against him, and his fingers brushed her powdery skin. "You know I'll miss you."

She snuggled closer, and he yearned to keep her there forever. But tonight was his turn to be honest. "In fact I'll make my confession. I would've asked you to join me on the Cape, but I haven't told my mother how I feel about you. I made our relationship sound casual when we talked. I thought telling her in person was better. Can you believe it? I'm ashamed of myself."

A pink flush rose up her neck, and she raised her head to face him. She pressed her hand to his cheek. "If this is confession night, let me join you. I haven't mentioned you to my brother and his wife. Their attitudes have been a little strained, and I'm waiting for a better time to talk to them."

Neither of them knew how to handle all that was going on. Brad surveyed Sally's face. She looked so fragile tonight, her long dark lashes lifting shyly to reveal her glistening green eyes. He lowered his lips to hers and raised his hand, caressing her cheek. Then he glided his hand to her delicate neck where his fingers tangled gently in her shining, soft hair.

When he felt ready to burst, all control crumbling around him, he forced his aching lips to leave hers and curved his arms around her, feeling her heart beating in rhythm with his own. "I'd better stop right now, or I won't stop at all."

"I don't want you to stop." She raised her lashes, uncovering her misted eyes. "But I know we must."

Brad forced himself to rise. For distraction, he grabbed the poker and jabbed at the glowing logs. He waited until his emotions had ebbed, and then he turned back to her. "I'd better get going. We leave early tomorrow, and I have lots to do."

She rose and returned to his arms. He felt her slender body blend into his own, and he wondered how one person could cause so many sensations to tear through him. She hugged him freely and, for the first time, kissed his eyelids and the tip of his nose, before placing her soft lips against his.

The kiss was gentle and fleeting, but she offered it eagerly. She stepped back, leaving one arm wrapped around his back. "Listen, have a wonderful time, and I'll be right here when you get back."

"You'd better be. I don't want some handsome man plying

you with his charm." He stood before her, their hands joined.

"I don't know any handsome men but you."

With shivers of yearning, he opened the door, promising to call her, and hurried to his car.

eight

When Brad walked out the door, Sally wanted to kick herself. She knew her mother would be rolling over in her grave if she heard her. Another fib. Ron was a handsome man—but not one Brad needed to worry about.

For the next few days, she relived their parting, and she asked herself over and over why she avoided mentioning the surprise party and Ron. Guilt? Fear he would think she was being vindictive? A ball of uncertainty bounced back and forth in her head.

Yet after all her worries, the party for Darby's engagement was wonderful. As always, Ron was a gentleman. On the way home, she casually told him about Brad during their conversation, and though surprise showed on his face, he listened with quiet acceptance. Why hadn't she been as honest with Brad?

Feeling sorry for herself wouldn't help a thing, and on Sunday after church, Sally solicited Ed's help to put up the Christmas tree later in the week with the promise of pizza and homemade cookies. He eagerly accepted.

Sally stopped by a tree lot and selected an old-fashioned balsam with sparse branches leaving spaces for large bulbs and other tree ornaments. Then a couple days before Christmas, she lay on the floor with Ed standing above her, gripping the sticky tree branch.

"Okay, hold it steady," Sally instructed, as she wound the screws of the stand tightly against the tree. "There. Let go, and see if it's okay."

As Ed removed his grip, the tree moved only slightly, and Sally breathed a sigh. "I think it's fine."

She crawled from under the tree and stood up. When they stepped back, Ed's guffaw filled the room before Sally burst into laughter.

"Looks like that leaning tower of Pizza," Ed chortled. The tree tilted noticeably to the right.

"That's *Pisa,* Ed, as if you didn't know." She gave his shoulder a poke and crawled beneath the tree for the second time, and after much readjusting, they gave up.

"This tree's a little like me, Sally. It has a mind of its own." He clamped his hand on her shoulder. "I think we ought to give the thing its rights."

"Rights," Sally said, arching her eyebrow. "It sure does have its *rights*."

The tree with its predominate tilt stood proudly, and with Christmas music playing in the background, Ed helped her haul out the decorations and she trimmed while he chomped on pizza. When the decorating was finished, Ed nibbled on a cookie while she admired the room lit only by the delicate lights of the Christmas tree.

Ed's sudden voice jolted her from her reverie. "So, where's your friend?"

"On the Cape. His mother's ill and couldn't travel."

Ed's knowing eyes studied her. "Thought you seemed a little down."

"It's that and more, Ed. His daughter Kelly hasn't quite warmed up to me yet. And my brother's so wary of me meeting anyone, I haven't told him about Brad. I keep praying and God isn't listening." She blinked the tears back behind her eyes. "Guess I have the holiday blues. Feeling sorry for myself."

"One thing I learned in my old age, Sally. You can't force

the issue. Things have a way of working out, and you need patience. And don't go blaming God. He's hearing those prayers, but maybe His answer is 'no' right now. Parents don't always agree with everything their children want. Sometimes, they know that things are worth waiting for." His kindly blue eyes sought hers. "Remember?"

She nodded, thinking of too many times as a child when her parents said no to her pleas.

"You just keep praying and listening. God's hearing you. And if I know fathers, after a while, they give you what you want just to shut you up." His laughter filled the room again.

His words brought a smile to Sally's face, and she gave him a huge bear hug. "Ed, what would I do without your sage wisdom?"

He chuckled, "Sally, you're getting along mighty fine. Just takes you a little longer, maybe." He patted her arm. "Don't lose hope—or faith. Things take time."

❧

The following Monday, Sally trudged to Davidson's, eagerly awaiting the Christmas holiday. In the morning, she came upon Darby in the copy room, concentrating on the pages flipping from the machine.

Sally put her arm around her friend's shoulder. "Hey, the engagement party was wonderful. You looked so surprised."

"Surprised! There's no word to describe how I felt. Astounded, maybe. We'd talked, but. . .flabbergasted, now there's a word." She laughed. "And speaking of flabbergasted, I was surprised to see you with Ron."

Sally faltered. "I wasn't really with him. He offered a ride and I tried to explain, but he wouldn't take my 'no.' I finally gave up. I did tell him I was seeing Brad."

Darby stared at her. "Was he disappointed? He often asks about you. I think he really likes you."

A soft flush rose on Sally's face. "I like him, too, but as a friend. I suppose I should confess that Brad's stolen my heart, Darby. We've no plans, no commitments, but he's all I think about. It feels so good, Darby. I'm feeling happy again."

"So, is this serious?"

"Too soon. I don't know. We're getting to know each other. We have fun. We're comfortable. Our values are similar— family, children, God. He makes me laugh and feel alive."

"Then enjoy it, Sally, but be careful. Keep an eye on your emotions. Remember what happened to Cassie Bellows in marketing?"

Sally's enthusiasm faded. She hadn't expected Darby to caution her. "What do you mean? I don't remember."

"You don't? She met some guy at a singles' club. Fell head over heels in love, and. . ."

Sally's heart fell. "Now I remember. They got married less than a year after they met and divorced in a shorter time." Sally scowled. "But I didn't meet Brad at a singles' club."

"I'm not saying you did. I mean, sometimes when we first tumble, we don't keep our heads on straight. You're no fool, Sally. You have lots and lots of time. What will be, will be. I'm happy for you. If Brad makes you happy, enjoy it. Just don't use Ron to make Brad jealous."

"I'm not." Sally snapped her response. "I've never used a person to hurt someone else. All I know is how I feel with Brad—safe and cared about. It's wonderful."

"Then be gentle with Ron. He's a good friend. I know you won't hurt him on purpose, but think before you act."

Sally tensed. Darby wasn't listening. "I said I told him about my feelings for Brad. I was honest with him."

"Good. If he realizes you're out of the picture, he'll find someone else. He's handsome."

"And nice, I know. There's a girl out there who'll love

him. It's just not me."

Confusion rattled through her. Why wasn't anyone thrilled for her when she mentioned Brad? All she heard from her family and now her friend were warnings. She was still hiding her feelings. What was wrong with her? If she truly loved him, wouldn't she sing his praises to the sky?

Returning to her desk, Sally found an envelope with her name printed on it, tucked under the computer keyboard. She lifted the flap and pulled out a note handwritten in a bold flourish. She scanned to the bottom, her pulse pounding. *Steve.*

Immediately, her hand trembled. *Why? What have I done?* The words blurred on the page.

> *What a scamp! You told me you aren't ready for dating. Tell the truth next time. I saw you at Aunt Fanny's. Don't tell me the guy's your brother. Save a little of that romance for me.*

The note dropped from her trembling hand. She stared at it lying on the floor, picked it up. Wadding the offensive paper into a ball, she threw it in the wastebasket. She had to do something about him.

On second thought, she retrieved the note and tucked it into her pocket. Hurrying down the hall, she entered Darby's office. Though preoccupied, as Sally flew into the room, Darby looked up.

"I know you're busy, but look at this." Sally handed her the note. Darby smoothed out the wrinkles and scanned the paper.

"Yep, he's weird." She faked a grin.

Sally pulled up a chair and sat beside her. "I don't know what to do about him. Most anyone looking at the note would think I'm silly. He isn't threatening me, but he makes me nervous. I have to get him to leave me alone."

"Talk to Jim. He can force Steve's hand. It's sexual harassment, I would say."

"It's only right I talk to Steve first. I can't say he's harassing me if I don't let him know how I feel. I just have to get the courage."

She paused for a second, her thoughts racing. The Bible said if you're offended by someone, talk to them. She had to work up the courage somehow. Being single was the pits.

Sally looked back at Darby. "I wish I understood him. I'd think a million women'd die for a chance to date him. Why me?"

"Because you don't want him, probably. Some people like a challenge. Chase him. He'll probably run like a rabbit."

"I'd rather be miserable."

Darby snickered and returned the note.

Sally crumpled it for the second time and tossed it into Darby's wastebasket. "That's what I think of Mr. Wall's little memo. Thanks for listening. I needed a shoulder to cry on."

"Anytime," Darby called after her.

Sally hurried back to her desk, thinking about Steve's note. Since Davidson Electric would close for the holiday, she decided to talk with him after the new year. Cowardice was becoming her specialty.

❧

On Christmas Eve after the worship service, Sally invited Alice and Ed to come for hot cider and desserts. Ed acted like a child when it came to the Christmas gifts. For the past two years they had exchanged small gifts. This year he saved hers until the end. It was larger than the rest, and although she knew it was from Ed, she was sure that Alice helped him wrap it. The gift looked elegant in deep green foil tied with a large plaid Christmas ribbon.

"Guess we know who this one is for." Ed chuckled and handed Sally the package.

She took it from him and gently slid off the beautiful ribbon. She removed the paper and lifted the box lid. "Oh, Ed. I said you should keep this. It's so pretty, and it holds all your family photos. You shouldn't have."

Sally looked down at the charming old photograph album in the delicate greens and pinks that Ed found in the trunk of his attic. Her eyes welled with tears.

Alice patted her hand. "Ed knew you'd like it, Sally."

"And don't you worry. Alice and I went to a little shop in town and found a replacement, not nearly so pretty, but it'll hold some of my old pictures. I wanted you to have this one, and I even left a few old photos in it. For the life of me, I have no idea who the folks are, so it will add a little authenticity to the album."

As always, Ed made Sally laugh. "I love it." She leaned over and kissed him on the cheek.

"See," he said to Alice. "It was worth it, right?"

Alice gave him a poke.

Sally looked through the leafs of the album, examining the shapes and sizes of slots for the pictures. "You know, if I remember correctly, I have a few old pictures from my parents' memorabilia in my attic. I haven't looked at them in years."

The album gave her a new idea. She could spend Christmas Day rummaging through the attic. She had no idea what she might find there. And best of all, she could pass the time waiting for Brad's phone call.

&

On Christmas Day Sally attended Christmas worship and, later in the day, plowed through the attic, looking for the old photographs. In the memorabilia, Sally found an old doll, her report cards in a manila envelope, and a packet of wonderful old letters tied with a traditional blue ribbon. She spent the rest of the afternoon reading the old letters and gazing at the tintype photographs.

Sally felt apprehensive, waiting for Brad's call. She kept her eye on the clock, and the clock hands pointed to seven in the evening when the telephone rang. She jumped with anticipation and hurried to answer it.

nine

"Merry Christmas."

Brad closed his eyes when he heard her voice. "Merry Christmas, Sally.

"I'm so glad you called. How's your visit? How are the kids?"

She sounded happy, and his tension faded. "The kids are great. Mother coddles them, and they need the attention. It makes Janet's absence easier. At least, it seems that way."

"I hoped it would. So, how's your mother?"

"Fine. She's sorry she didn't get to meet you."

If it hadn't been for the children, he might have avoided telling his mother about his growing feelings for Sally. He feared she'd think he got involved with a woman too soon. But Danny blurted out Sally's name over and over with Kelly coming in second, and his mother didn't miss a word. To his delight, she sounded pleased.

Yet her enthusiasm also carried the usual mother's caution. "Just don't rush into anything, Brad. You've been lonely. Don't mistake passion for real love." He was sure he hadn't, but he would keep her warning tucked somewhere in his subconscious.

He'd spent a lot of time thinking while he was gone. They needed to deal with their fears if they were ever going to make their relationship work. He was as guilty as Sally.

"I really miss you, Sally. A lot."

"I miss you too," she whispered.

The urge to get back to her overwhelmed him. "We'll be

here a few more days. Mom's kept us busy, but I'm looking forward to getting home."

"I'm anxious to see you."

He didn't care what anyone said. How could these feelings not be love?

"Brad, you'll never guess what happened since you've been gone. Darby and Eric are engaged."

"Engaged. Great. They're a nice couple."

"I knew before you left, but I was sworn to secrecy."

"You knew about what?"

"Eric planned a surprise dinner party for close friends and family and proposed there. In front of everyone. It was nice."

Disappointment edged through him. Promises aren't meant to be kept from. . .from who? Boyfriends? Husbands? What was he to Sally? "Sorry I wasn't there to go with you."

"Me, too," she mumbled.

Sally's voice sounded strange. He had to ask, but he wasn't sure he wanted to hear the answer. "You didn't go alone, did you?"

He heard her inhale. "Ron Morton helped Eric make the calls. He offered to pick me up. You remember him, don't you?"

Naturally, he remembered. "Sure. From Darby's birthday party."

"Uh-huh." She rushed on. "They made me promise I wouldn't tell Darby. I had a terrible time keeping quiet."

"I bet you did." He sensed tension between them, but he didn't know if it were his or hers. "I'm glad you had someone to go with. It's more fun."

The line was silent until he continued. "Well, I don't want to say good-bye, but I better get back to the family. I really miss you. I'll call as soon as we get home."

"I can't wait, Brad. Have a safe trip. . .and give my best to your mom and hug the kids for me."

When he hung up, he felt irritated. The tension that filled the empty airwaves made talking impossible. His hair bristled when she casually mentioned Ron.

If she were trying to make him jealous, she had done a good job, but he didn't like that either. He rolled his shoulders, feeling the tension move from his neck down his spine. They would have to talk when he got home.

ⱥ

When Bill and Sue returned from Florida, they invited Sally for dinner. Carrie talked incessantly, listing every gift she received and detailing every event.

Sally enjoyed the evening until Sue asked if she had plans for New Year's Eve. "I'm staying home." She needed to introduce the subject of Brad, and Sue's question gave her the opportunity. "I would have plans except the man I'd like to be with is—"

Bill, who was only half listening, cut her off. "I'm glad you're taking it easy, Sis. Sue and I think you should take your time getting back into the social whirl. Too many people jump into relationships while they're still grieving and make big mistakes."

Sally winced. "But Bill, I'm not—"

"Right," Sue said, "and you know what men want, Sally. Many of them just want to take advantage of your loneliness. Getting involved with someone now could lead to nothing but trouble."

Sally froze. How could she tell them about Brad now? Better to keep it quiet than hear their disdain.

"Darby's warned me about the plight of single women." She hoped the comment would halt the subject. "And speaking of Darby, she and Eric are engaged. He invited a few friends for a surprise dinner and asked her in front of the whole crowd."

Bill laughed. "Wow, how embarrassing if she'd said no."

"He must have been pretty sure she'd say yes, silly," Sue said, "or he wouldn't have asked her that way."

Sally sighed, relieved she'd sidetracked them. She'd wait a long time before she'd mention Brad.

The conversation didn't return to New Year's Eve, but their words kept coming back to her, and Darby's warning came to mind. *Remember what happened to Cassie Bellows in marketing? She fell head over heels in love, and. . .* Her thoughts would remain private from now on. She would savor the pleasure and deal with the pain alone until she knew she could handle everyone's negative attitudes. Was there one person who'd be happy for her?

こ

Sally sat alone on New Year's Eve, watching the ball drop in Times Square and thinking about Brad. As always, thoughts of him warmed her. Still, icy fear crept in to cool her spirit. She lost one love. Would her relationship with Brad be a blossoming flower that also died on the vine?

The more she thought, the more troubled she became. Brad had children, and they added problems. How could he get on with his life when the children hadn't? The situation was frustrating and mind-boggling. The answer seemed to rest on time.

On January third, Sally returned to work, facing the year-end inventory and knowing that she must talk to Steve. She had put the confrontation off long enough. Looking for a neutral location, she settled on the company cafeteria.

When she entered the lunchroom, Steve was alone at a table. She wanted to get the whole thing over with. She breathed deeply, harnessing her courage, and marched forward bravely. "May I join you?"

Before he spoke, he examined her from feet to face. "My

pleasure." He rose, pulling out a chair. His unusual attempt at chivalry embarrassed her. Steve returned to his seat and stared at her until she flushed. He appeared amused.

Sally bolstered her courage. "I've been wanting to speak to you since I found your note."

"My note?"

She had no desire to play games with him.

"Oh, my note. It was so long ago I nearly forgot."

"Steve, I'm asking you to please understand that I'm not interested in seeing you socially. I prefer keeping my work separate from my private life."

"I bet you do." His mouth curved into a smirk, and he leaned across the table. "I like to see you with fire in your eyes," he said in a breathy murmur. "It looks good on you. Real spunky." He slurred his words.

Sally felt her courage failing. "There are many women who'd probably enjoy your attention, Steve. I'm not one of them. I don't appreciate it at all."

"*He* must be quite a man. I admire him."

Sally frowned, confused by his comment. "What are you talking about?"

"The friend you were with at Aunt Fanny's. He must be quite a man to keep you happy. You're a little spitfire."

Sally rose, her voice an angry whisper. "Listen, Steve, I wanted to be civil, but you don't understand. I'm not interested in you. I never will be. You're harassing me, and if you don't leave me alone, I'll be forced to do something about it." She spun around and darted from the lunchroom.

à

When Brad arrived home on Tuesday, he dropped the luggage and rushed to the telephone before he unpacked. "It's good to know you're only a few miles away instead of hundreds," Brad said. "How about dinner? I can't wait to see you."

All her feelings melted away and a smile spread across her face. "I'm ready now."

"Do you mind if I bring the kids? Or I can get a sitter. Maybe that would be best."

"No, please bring the children. I've missed them."

Her words filled him with joy. "Great. They're anxious to see you."

Amazing, he thought. The tension seemed gone. She'd forgiven him for missing Christmas with her. "Great. I'll pick you up about five and then drop them back home before the meeting."

Their "welcome home" dinner was filled with the children's chatter, and Brad hardly had time to say a word. He controlled his own eager greeting, knowing he and Sally would have to wait until they were alone. But after dinner, Sally handed the children gifts she'd purchased for them, and then opened their package to her. She pinned the guardian angel pin to her lapel, and tears glistened in her eyes.

⁂

Near the end of January, Sally and Brad headed for their last meeting of the grief group. The participants clustered together in talkative groups like graduation day, reminiscing about their first meeting and the progress they'd made. For Sally and Brad, the memories held special meaning.

Jack ended with the topic, "A Time to Love." Brad held Sally's hand, squeezing lightly as he listened to Jack's words. "Love does not have limits. Think of God's love for us. It never runs out. God loves us with fullness and completeness. No one is loved more than another. We are loved equally. So we may love again, not diminishing the love we had, but a new love—equal, full, and complete—may grow in your lives."

Jack words rattled through Brad. He remembered feeling

guilty when Sally first came to the house, as if he were cheating on Janet by sharing their children and home with another woman. But that had changed. His love was boundless and growing daily.

Jack finished, "Our loved ones helped create the persons we are. A new love is only an extension of the love we had. Our departed loved ones continue to live in us as we live in God and in each other. May our love for one another and God's love shine through us always." When Jack finished, the room thundered with spontaneous applause.

The discussion group session flew by. Telephone numbers were exchanged, prayers were offered and requested, and finally, hugs and good-byes were given. Brad and Sally walked out together into the surprisingly mild January night.

Waving to others, they ambled toward the car. Brad held Sally's hand and leaned into her shoulder, feeling familiar and loving. When they slid into the car, he wrapped his arm around her, caressing her shoulder. "I know our relationship is only months old, Sally, but I want you to know you make me feel whole again."

Sally looked into his eyes without speaking, but when Brad lowered his lips to hers, he needed no words. Their lips met tenderly, breathlessly, like a compelling love song. She yielded to the kiss, returning freely what he gave to her. The kiss lay gentle and sweet on his lips and on his heart. Brad lingered, brushing kisses on the end of her nose and her eyelids. She raised her lips to meet his once again, and his former worries melted away.

Her voice came like a whisper. "You mean so much to me, Brad. I've been trying to sort through it all. I didn't think that I could feel this way again. In many ways, it seems I've known you for a lifetime."

He nestled her within his arms, holding her as if he would

never let go. When he relaxed, easing against the seat cushion, he gazed steadily into her eyes that glistened with tears. "I love you, Sally."

"I've been afraid to call it love, Brad. Whatever it is, it's wonderful—but it scares me."

He didn't tell her he felt scared at times, too. "We have time. All the time in the world."

Headlights from another car flashed past the window, and Brad noticed two men standing next to their cars, watching them. He pointed to them. "If we don't leave soon, we'll have a crowd volunteering to give us a push. I imagine they think my car won't start." They laughed as he started the car and drove from the lot.

ten

On February first, Sally dealt quietly with the second anniversary of Tim's death. She climbed into her car alone and drove to the cemetery, her thoughts stirring inside her head. On her lapel, she attached the guardian angel pin, the Christmas present from Kelly and Danny. In her gloved hands, she carried a piece of German chocolate cake. In a way, the cake seemed foolish, but Tim loved German chocolate cake and she could think of nothing else to bring to him on a cold, wintry day. She traversed the frozen grass and stood over his grave.

The stone was free of snow, and she read the inscription. *Loving Husband, Timothy Ronald Newgate, April 7, 1958 to February 1, 1996.* Sally bent down, tracing her finger along the letters carved into the gray granite, for once controlling her emotions.

Feeling foolish, she placed the cake on the grave. "Well Tim, my love, you may think a piece of cake is rather silly. I realize this isn't a celebration—and not exactly a regular party, but it's a gift from my heart. I know heaven is filled with wonderful things, but I'm not sure if heaven has really good German chocolate cake. I know how much you love it."

Her eyes puddled with tears, and she pushed them back, closing them for a moment to gain her composure.

A large pine tree stood nearby, and Sally wandered over and leaned against its sturdy trunk. She spoke aloud, feeling comfort in the sense of real conversation. In her memory, she could see Tim grinning at her when she did something silly.

"Tim, I need to talk to you. I hope you know I'm okay. In fact, I'm doing pretty good now. That's what I want to tell you about. I never thought it would happen, but I've met a really wonderful man—with two children, a girl and a boy, Kelly and Danny."

Her lips trembled, and she stopped speaking to calm her emotions. "Brad means a lot to me. Love is what I think it is, and I want you to know. I cherish the years we had, but I have a lot more love to give—enough, even, for those two lovely children who need a mom. Knowing you, I imagine you're happy I've found someone. I know I'd have wanted you to fall in love again. . ."

She swallowed to stem the sorrow creeping into her voice. ". . .and have the children we never had. Oh, Tim, I think that was the second worst part, not having even one little piece of you with me."

This time she let the tears fall, rolling in warm rivulets down her cheeks until they turned to icy dampness beneath her chin. "I'm not going to stand here and cry like a baby. I feel sorry for myself. And I'm scared."

She walked back to the grave and patted the headstone. "I'm going to go before I get too morbid, but I'll leave the cake, and I want you to know that I love you." She turned away and hurried to her car.

≈

In the beginning of March, Sally received a surprise telephone call from her old friend, Elaine. It had been months since she had heard from her. The hurt still lingered over the distance between them following Tim's death, and when Elaine invited her out to dinner, Sally was pleased.

But the dinner and friendship felt different and strained.

When they returned to the house, Sally made coffee, and their conversation turned to children.

Elaine stared thoughtfully into her coffee cup. "Mark and I are hoping to have a baby soon, did I mention that?"

"No, but it would be wonderful." Sally pushed back her pangs of envy. "Tim and I decided to try again—just before the accident."

"Sally, I feel so bad. I know this has been so hard for you, and I haven't been a good friend."

Sally wanted to agree and say, *Right. You haven't been a good friend to me,* but she couldn't. Attacking Elaine served no purpose but to create guilt. Guilt wasn't productive, but sharing was. If anyone should be happy for her, Elaine should.

"You've been away Elaine. And I've made new friends." Sally took a deep breath, bolstering courage. "One has become really special, a widower from my grief group with two little kids. He's wonderful, and I care about him and his children. Kelly's seven and Danny's five. They miss their mother dreadfully."

Elaine glared, and her voice took on an edge. "You seem to know him well. Is this serious?"

An icy sensation shivered through Sally's body. "I don't know, Elaine. It's a fairly new relationship. He loves me, and I. . .I love him."

Elaine's voice sliced through Sally. "I'm surprised at you, Sally. Tim hasn't been gone that long. I can't believe you're involved with someone already!"

"Elaine, I didn't say I was involved—not the way you make it sound. We're good friends. We understand each other. We share feelings and dreams." Sally clenched her fists, her nails digging into the palms of her hands. "I didn't die, Elaine. Tim did. It's been two years. I've felt dead long enough. I need to live, and I'd think you, of all people, would want me to."

Sally couldn't believe that she was saying these things to Elaine. Anger and frustration boiled inside her. Tears clung to her cheeks. She raised her gaze heavenward, remembered what God expected of Christians. A renewed peace swept over her and her anger subsided like a leaf caught on a dying gust of wind. She loved Elaine. No more hurt was needed for anyone. There had been enough for a lifetime.

"Oh, Elaine, I'm so sorry. I can't believe I talked to you like that. It was hard, Elaine, and I needed you so badly. You were always my best friend, the person who I could tell my deepest thoughts—and you always understood. I don't have you anymore. You're too far away, and my other best friend was too far away, too—he died."

Elaine looked on, pale-faced, mouth agape as Sally brushed the tears from her eyes. "I've made new friends and picked up the pieces of my life. I can't sit in the house and die, too. I'm young. Tim wouldn't want me to die. I know he wouldn't."

Sally tried to compose her voice and her emotions, but her body quivered with depths of stored, repressed feelings. They were unleashed like wild animals. Her honesty and hurt bounded across the space between her and Elaine.

Elaine covered her face in her hands and wept. "Sally, please forgive me. How could I say that to you?" Pulling a tissue from her handbag, she dabbed at her eyes. "You're right. I've been sitting in Bay City with my husband and my new life. You've been here alone. I am so sorry, Sally. I wish we had talked long ago."

When she rose to leave, Sally held her arms open, drained and weary, and they clung together like the old friends they had always been. Though their differences had been settled, Sally faced the truth. Few people understood her feelings for Brad. People measured her feelings based on their concept of time and their measurement of love. Sally wanted to scream to heaven, *Lord, answer me. Tell me what is right. You're silent when I need to hear Your voice. You've said everything has a season and a purpose under heaven. Lord, when is my season?*

ka.

Easter came early in April. Sally took stock of the situation. If God wasn't going to help her, she needed to help herself. She'd allowed everyone's opinion to guide her, and she'd hidden Brad from Bill and Sue. The time had come to deal with the issue. She invited Brad and the children to her home for Easter dinner. Brad and her family needed to meet.

Yet, despite her resolve, the words of family and friends banged unpleasantly in her thoughts. Elaine, Bill and Sue, and Darby, people who should want her happiness offered her only fears. She remembered Darby's comments. *Sometimes when we first tumble, we don't keep our heads on straight.* Is that what had happened? Was she throwing all good sense out the window?

Easter morning when Sally rose, she looked through the bay window in the dining room to study the weather. A beautiful day appeared with a sky clear and the sun like a bright golden ball.

Her mother always told her the sun danced for joy on Easter morning. As a child, she hoped to awaken early enough to watch the sun dance, but she never did. She smiled, remembering her mother and her childhood Easters. Might the sun dance today in her brother's eyes when he saw her happiness?

Brad took the children to their own church for Easter services while Bill and his family joined Sally at Good Hope. The Easter music soared with of the strains of "Christ has Arisen! Hallelujah!" Choirs sang and a brass ensemble added their festive sounds to the hymns and anthems. But Sally felt empty of the joy and looked to the cross, wondering why God ignored her prayers.

When Sally arrived home, the sweet spicy aroma of the ham baking slowly in the oven drifted through the house, whetting everyone's appetite. Sally offered coffee and bagels to everyone and then distracted Carrie with a new picture book. She took advantage of the quiet moment to prepare Bill and Sue for Brad and the children.

Bill's face soured. "It's your life, Sally. You do what you want. But a man who's only been alone for a year doesn't seem like a wise choice. You'll step into his life and mess his kids up good. They haven't adjusted to their mother's loss yet. Then you come along and leave them. Seems pretty tacky to me."

Sally's voice caught in her throat, and she struggled to keep tears from her eyes. "I'm not planning to hurt the children. I'm very fond of them, and—"

"No one said you've planned it, Sally," Sue said. "Children get used to you being around and then when you leave, there's another hole in their lives. You certainly don't think this will be a lasting relationship with this man, do you? You know he's a new widower."

Her eyebrows raised, and Sally felt herself sink into the chair cushion, beaten back by their words. "I don't know where this is leading. We're giving it time."

Bill's voice rose, and Sally noticed Carrie looked at them with curiosity. "Well, I should hope so. You had a great marriage to Tim. I sure don't want to see you land in divorce court a year or two after you marry this guy. Use your head."

Shocked, Sally's anger rose. She and Bill rarely had words, and today it was the last thing she wanted, but she snapped her response. "Divorce? Never. I'm sorry you don't approve. I'm not planning to jump off the deep end with any decision.

And I *have* used my head." *And my heart,* she added to herself.

Sue watched, her gaze darting from one to the other. "Let's not get riled here. We'll make the best of it. Bill, it's Sally's decision, not ours."

"All I ask," Sally added, "is that you make Brad and his children feel welcome."

Sue turned to Sally. "This is your home, Sally. We'll certainly be cordial, won't we, Bill?"

Bill nodded his head and shrugged. He rose and snapped on the television to a golf tournament.

A noise sounded in the driveway, and Carrie rose from her book, glancing out the window. "Your company's here," Carrie called out as she ran toward the door.

Sally watched Brad and the children come up the walk to the porch. Beneath her coat, Kelly was donned in a sea-green dress, the same color glinting in her eyes, with a floral print ruffle at the hem and neck. Danny, looking the image of his father, sported gray slacks and a navy blue sport coat.

Sally's aching heart lurched with love, and she ushered them in, trying to hide the fear that spread through her. With the introductions, Bill shook hands halfheartedly and turned his face back to the television set. Carrie seemed shy for a moment, but when Danny noticed her new storybook, she showed him the pictures, and they sat together on the floor. Kelly stood back and watched in silence.

"Kelly," Sally said, "would you like to help me in the kitchen? I could use an assistant."

Kelly shrugged, giving the other children a sidelong glance. "I guess so." She followed Sally into the kitchen. "I'm more grown-up than Danny and Carrie."

Sally agreed, then gave Kelly the silverware for the table and the child headed off to do her job. As Sally pulled the ham from the oven, Brad walked into the kitchen.

"Smells wonderful. Much better than the unpleasant aura in the living room." He placed his hands on Sally's lower neck muscles and massaged. "You're as tense as a wound-up spring."

"I know. I just told Bill about you today. Sorry, I should have done it sooner, but I'm a terrible coward. He promised to be civil."

"Good. And I promise to do the same." He stepped back as she pulled the ham from the oven. "And time for a taste test."

Sally gave him a quick grin, setting the roaster on trivets. "How about if you maneuver the ham into the stand there?" She pointed to a metal holder. "You can be in charge of slicing."

"I'd be delighted. With the knife in my hand, I'll know it's not headed for my back." He gave her a teasing smile. She grimaced and he quickly added, "Just kidding."

Kelly returned to the kitchen and hesitated for a moment in the doorway and then continued into the room. "I'm an assistant, Daddy. I'm setting the table."

"Let me see." He wiped his hands and followed her into the dining room. Sally heard him talking to her from the other room. "You've done a very nice job, as always—like Mom taught you."

When they returned to the kitchen, Kelly's face reflected she was pleased he had compared her to her mother. Kelly continued her tasks, as Brad sliced the ham, garnishing the dish with pineapple slices. Sally placed the potato casserole in a protective wicker basket and dished up the vegetables.

When the table was ready, she called the family. Bill and Sue wandered into the dining room, cordial as they had promised, but restrained. They gathered around the table and bowed their heads for prayer. Though conversation seemed stilted, they ate with relish, and Sally was grateful.

After dinner, the children were eager for an activity and sat on the floor looking at the Candyland game that Kelly had brought along. When Alice and Ed arrived to join them for dessert, their presence eased the tension, and conversation flowed more freely.

When the pies were eaten, Sally carried the dishes and leftover desserts into the kitchen. She was at the sink rinsing dishes when Brad walked up behind her, putting his arms around her waist. He kissed her hair, and she turned to face him.

"You smell just as good as that cinnamon apple pie," he murmured.

"I take that as quite a compliment."

He slid his hands up and down her arms, looking deeply into her eyes, then embraced her, lowering his lips to hers with a kiss, deep and loving. Brad moved his arms tenderly along her back, and she felt wonderful being near him. When their kiss ended, she remained enfolded in his arms with her head resting on his shoulder.

Brad's voice was hushed. "Sally, I want to tell you. . ." Before he could finish, a sound stopped him, and when he swung around, Kelly stood in the dining room doorway, a game piece from her hand rolling across the floor. She stared at them, unmoving.

eleven

Brad rushed toward Kelly, but she pivoted and ran into the dining room. Brad followed her and held her in his arms as she sobbed. "Kelly, Sally is my friend. She's helping all of us from being so sad. We have fun again like a new—"

But Kelly's words shattered the silence. "But she's not my mother. I don't want a different mother. I want my own."

Brad's heart lurched, tears filling his eyes for her pain. "I know, sweetheart, but. . ." What could he say to ease her fears and sense of loss?

They'd been so careful, doing everything to avoid upsetting the children. How could he have been so thoughtless today? He knew Kelly was nearby, but in his emotions, he had forgotten.

When Kelly quieted, he looked into her face. "Wait here a minute, and I'll get our things so we can leave." Brad left the dining room feeling tense and drawn. He returned to the kitchen where Sally waited, staring at the doorway, her eyes wide and filled with the evidence of tears.

"I'm so sorry, Sally," he whispered.

"Me, too. Is she okay?"

"She will be, but I think we'd better go. I hate to leave on such a note, but it's best. Would you call Danny in here so we can leave through the back? You can explain after we're gone and give my apologies to everyone."

"Brad, I feel bad, too, but isn't sneaking away a bit dramatic? Danny's having fun, and—"

"Sally, I don't want to upset Kelly any more than she's

already upset. It's better if we leave quietly."

"But won't leaving so quickly give her the impression we're wrong to care about each other? We've tried to be thoughtful, Brad. How long will it take for them to accept me?"

"It will take as long as it takes. I'm sorry you feel that way. Please ask Danny to come in here."

Sally's face registered shock, but she did as he asked. Brad hurried back to the dining room and, protectively, guided Kelly to the kitchen as Sally returned with a confused Danny.

"Why do we have to go, Daddy?" Disappointment filled his face. "We're playing Candyland."

"I know, son, but Kelly doesn't feel well. We have to go home now. You can play the game another day."

Danny pouted as Brad herded the children out the back door. Sally stared after them, pale and silent.

⁂

Monday at Davidson's, Sally was in the midst of chaos. She couldn't get Brad out of her mind. She knew the children needed time for adjustment, but that's what she thought they were doing, moving slowly and cautiously. How much time did it take? She felt impatient. She wanted to show her feelings for Brad openly. Yet, now, they'd hurt Kelly.

She expected Brad to protect his children. But yesterday, she felt alienated from him, as if he were ashamed of their feelings for each other. As the thought trudged through, she remembered her own delay in sharing her feelings with Bill. She realized her error.

Along with her personal worries, Davidson's was involved in a company inventory and a buyout transaction. Moving quickly was important. Sally agreed to stay late to help complete the information necessary for negotiations.

When her telephone extension buzzed in the afternoon, she controlled the irritation in her voice. The caller was Brad.

"Hope this isn't inconvenient," he said cautiously. "I've been thinking of you all day and didn't get a chance to call last night."

"How did things go?" Their first real argument lingered in her mind, a mixture of hurt and frustration.

"First, I want to apologize, Sally. I acted like an idiot. I should have considered your feelings too. We've done everything we can to help the kids adjust, and I don't know what else to do."

"I didn't mean to sound cold and unfeeling, Brad. I'm sorry that it happened, too. Later I thought about Bill and Sue and how I've behaved. We have our own problems accepting the changes in our lives, worried about what others think. Then we have the children's problems. I'm beginning to think our problems will never end."

"Please don't be discouraged. We'll work things out." Brad paused a moment. Sally wondered if he believed what he said. Then Brad broke the silence. "When I got home last night, I got Danny distracted with his toys. He was upset because he had to leave your house. With him busy I explained things to Kelly. I said you and I are good friends—that you care about all of us. I stressed *all*. I told her you made me happy and helped me get over my sadness. When I said that, I saw the fear in her eyes—like I had already forgotten her mother. I assured her that I would always love Janet."

"Did she understand? Even if she did, I'm sure she felt betrayed."

"I imagine—in her eyes, I betrayed her and her mother by kissing you. Oh, Sally, this is so difficult. I feel terrible. Last night, I didn't think about Kelly being in the next room. I looked at you and did what my heart told me to do. I kissed you. Now, we have a mess again. I feel like you do. I'm losing patience." His sigh echoed over the phone line. "It'll work out."

"I know. We had made good progress—until yesterday."

"Could we get together tonight or tomorrow night? I can get Katie to baby-sit. We need to talk and decide where we go from here—what we do next. I need ideas. I want to help the kids, but I can't stop living, Sally."

"Brad, I'm working tonight and probably tomorrow night. We have some complicated stuff going on here. Maybe I can get off by eight tomorrow. We could have a late dinner together."

"That would be great. I hate to put you in the middle of my family problems, but. . ."

"I *am* in the middle. You didn't put me there. I joined right in, so I'm responsible, too. I care about the kids, Brad."

"I know you care, or I wouldn't ask you. Maybe tomorrow we can think of something."

❧

Sally and Brad agreed upon a plan—quality time for her and Kelly, just the two of them. Sally suggested taking her to lunch and asking her to help select a birthday gift for Carrie. A few days later, Brad had eased the idea into Kelly's mind and following a personal telephone call from Sally, Kelly agreed.

The child waited at the door when Sally pulled into the driveway the next day, and they headed for Kelly's restaurant choice, Big Top Burger. The fast-food restaurant offered special meals packaged for children with a surprise toy inside, and Kelly was collecting the miniature dolls. With their meals ordered at the counter, they found seats.

Sally had used every piece of parenting technique she could muster, praying she would move cautiously. "Do you like to shop, Kelly? Your daddy says you are very helpful."

"Uh-huh, my mom liked me to shop with her. I pushed the cart at the grocery store. And put things in the basket."

"That was helpful. Your mom was smart to think of taking you along."

She nodded, her bright curls bouncing. "My mom was smart."

"I've never had a girl to help me shop before. I'm glad you came with me. When I was your age, I liked to help my mom."

Kelly's gaze drifted to Sally's. "Do you help her now?"

"No, I can't anymore, Kelly. My mom died, just like yours."

"She did?" Kelly eyes widened in surprise. Then she frowned. "Did she get real sick, like my mommy did?"

"Yes, she did. My mom died about ten years ago. I really miss her."

"You do?" Again Kelly's eyes widened, this time with a question. The look washed over her face until finally she spoke. "Did you forget what she looks like?"

Sally was stunned at Kelly's question. Now, she fathomed the depth of Kelly's fears. "No, I'll never forget, Kelly. I have lots of pictures that I look at to remind me. I can even hear her voice in my head, telling me to eat so I don't get sick."

Kelly nodded as she listened. "My mom said I should eat all my vegetables." A silence settled over them. She looked at Sally, searching her face, soliciting trust before she confessed in a voice like a whisper, "Sometimes, I'm afraid I'll forget what she looks like."

Sally's heart ached. "You have pictures of her at home, don't you? Ask your daddy to give you a picture of your very own to put in your room. On your nightstand, maybe. Then you'll see her face before you go to bed at night and when you get up in the morning. That would be nice."

Kelly nodded. "Then I won't forget."

Sally heard her audible sigh of relief. "Oh, Kelly, sweetheart, you'll never forget. Moms are very special. No one takes a mom's place. No one would ever want to."

Kelly looked at Sally quizzically, her pretty green eyes searching Sally's face. Then, as if it were a new day, a smile curled on her lips, and she changed the subject.

They finished lunch and continued on to stores where Kelly pointed out games and clothes she thought Carrie might like. Sally made her purchases. As they left the department store, Sally eyed a display of small padded picture frames covered in delicate floral fabrics, perfect for a snapshot.

She lead the petite child to the display. "Kelly, do you like these?" She pointed to the frames. "You could pick one out for your mom's picture. I'd like to buy it for you."

Kelly's gaze riveted to the bright cloth frames. Taking her time, Kelly looked at each one, questioning if it were a design and color that her mother would like. Finally she made her selection. The clerk placed it in a bag, and Kelly carried the purchase herself, holding it against her chest like a precious gem. "Thank you for the present."

"You're very welcome." Sally said, giving her a hug. Kelly responded by hugging her back. They were friends again. "I have an idea. Let's go to my house. We can call your dad and Danny and have them come over for dinner. We could order pizza and make a salad."

"Okay. I'll call Daddy when we get to your house. And then we could play a game after our pizza. It's still at your house, isn't it?"

Sally could only nod. A lump formed in her throat. She looked at this dear child so recently sorrowful, now clinging to her parcel and jabbering about pizza and Candyland.

❧

Summer weather came quickly. In late May, the temperature stayed in the eighties. The beaches opened Memorial Day weekend, and Sally was packing a picnic lunch to take to the beach when the telephone rang.

"Sally, this is Elaine. I wanted to tell you in person, but I can't wait. We're expecting a baby."

"Oh, Elaine, I am so happy." Sally winced involuntarily, ashamed that she thought of herself. The feeling passed quickly, and her joy for Elaine and Mark returned. "Mark is ecstatic, I'm sure."

"Oh, you would think he did it all by himself. I get no credit." Silence hovered for a moment before she continued. "I'm still feeling bad about what I said, Sally. I hope you've forgiven me."

"Elaine, we all say things we wished we hadn't. You know I've forgiven you." She hadn't forgotten, however, and she wished she could. "Let me know if you're coming down this way again, and if I'm coming yours, I'll let you know."

The conversation ended on a congenial note, yet Sally rolled her shoulders to relieve the tension. Forgiveness was something she could give. Forgetting wasn't as easy, and she longed to erase the memory of that day from her mind.

ஃ

Brad arrived with the children early, eager to be on their way. If they were early enough, they could lay claim on a table in a choice location. The beaches were popular with the warm temperature, especially on Memorial Day weekend.

They found a parking spot that would be protected by shade later in the day. Gathering blankets, food basket, cooler, and swimming paraphernalia, he loaded up Sally and the children, and they headed for the picnic tables closest to the water.

The water felt cold even in the heat of the day. Danny walked in timidly, uncertain and cautious. Everyone but Brad yelled out and shivered as the icy liquid rolled up their bodies. He forced himself to be courageous, a bit of masculine pride, he admitted to himself, and he was the first to dive in, stifling his screams of icy anguish. Kelly followed, but didn't hold back from admitting the water was cold. Brad looked back toward the shore, and grinned. He'd left Sally in the shallow water to wade with Danny.

After lunch, Brad sent the children to play in the sand. He wanted to speak to Sally in private. She spread a blanket on the ground next to the picnic table and leaned against the bench. He spread out on his back looking at the fleecy wisps of clouds overhead.

"My friend Elaine called to tell me she and Mark are expecting a baby. Naturally, I'm thrilled for her, but I have to admit I had a twinge of jealousy."

Brad gazed at her face glowing in the sunlight and longed to say something to bring her peace of mind. They'd had difficult times dealing with their personal sorrows and struggling with Kelly. But things had finally begun to fall into place. Someday Sally would be a mother herself, and he prayed he would be the father of that baby.

He lay on the blanket in thoughtful silence, then grinned at her. "One of these days when you're waddling around with your belly out a mile, you'll wonder why you ever felt jealous." He rumpled her hair. "And I'm planning to stand by your side and laugh at you."

Though she attempted to act casual, a look of amazement crept across her face. "Thanks for your vote of confidence."

"No problem. In fact, I'm looking forward to it."

A blush rose on her cheeks, and he quieted his beating heart.

"You know, Brad, I probably never told you the whole story, and it's something that's caused me so much grief. I suppose I'm ashamed of myself."

Icy fear darted through him. "What, Sally?" *Nothing could be that bad.*

"When I had the miscarriage, Tim begged me to try again. He didn't just ask me, he begged. And I refused. I had no faith, and I was terribly ashamed of myself. Like I was inferior, even though I knew better."

He rested his hand on hers and felt the tremors race through her.

"After Tim died, I felt such shame and loss, not only for him, but for the child we might have had. I longed so much for one after he was gone. But then, it was too late."

He pressed her hand beneath his. "But it's not too late now, Sally. Forgive yourself. We all do foolish things we wish we could erase. You've grieved enough."

"I know, but I wanted to tell you."

"I'm glad you did." They sat in silence, and as the tension eased from her body, Brad continued. "So, let me tell you my news. I'm taking my vacation in July." He paused, looking for the children on the sand. Seeing them playing safely, he turned back to Sally. "I wanted to talk to you about your vacation. Do you have any plans yet?"

"Nothing yet." She eyed him, and he thought he saw a glimmer of hope reflected in her face. "What are you planning?"

"Well, that's what I wanted to talk to you about. I'm taking the kids to Cape Cod to visit my mom. She loves it when we come. It's wonderful there in the summer—the ocean, the quaintness." He saw he had piqued her interest. "I'd like you to come, too. I'll be gone nearly a month, but I'd like you to come for whatever time you can arrange. I've been talking to Mom about you, and she's anxious to meet you."

"Oh, now that's scary. You're taking me home to meet your mother?"

"Isn't that the first step?"

"That's what I'm afraid of."

Though she joked, Brad noted the heightened color in her cheeks and a sparkle in her eyes. She was pleased with the invitation.

"I could arrange a week, I imagine. It would give me time with the kids—and with you. I'd love it."

"A week would be wonderful. The kids and I'd be really happy, and it would make my mother happy, too."

"Well, let's not disappoint your mom." She gave him a coy smile.

ॐ

The next weeks flew by, and Brad stopped by before he left for the Cape. His mind hammered with things he wanted to share with Sally, but couldn't yet. He had to prepare her for them. He'd talk to her on the Cape.

"Brad, is something wrong? I feel like you're going to give me bad news or something."

He took her hand in his, rubbing her cool skin with his warm fingers. "Nothing's wrong. We haven't talked about us lately, and I guess I've been wondering where we're headed. Where do I stand in your life?"

"What brought this on?"

"Oh, I don't know. Maybe I'm getting melancholy knowing that I'm going away, and it'll be a couple of weeks before I'll see you again. I'm taking you to meet my mother, and I suppose I want to know if you care as much about me as I do about you."

She pressed his hand with hers. "Brad, you have no reason to wonder. I care about you more than any man I know. We've shared so much. We've helped each other through terrible times. Our lives are intertwined. No one is as important to me—just you and the kids."

"I wanted to hear you say that. I love you, Sally. I know you're a worrier. You wonder if we've known each other long enough to be sure about our feelings, but I don't think it has anything to do with time. It has to do with people. People who open themselves and share everything that's important." He looked deeply into her eyes, longing to read her mind.

She gazed back at him, this time her eyes more assured. "I am a worrier, I can't deny that. One day long ago, I asked Ed about being single after years of marriage, and he said something that's stayed with me. 'When the right person comes along, you'll know it. You won't ask questions. You'll know it.' And I do. I do love you, Brad."

A question lay on the tip of his tongue, but all he could force himself to say was a hint of his real concern. "Enough to go to the ends of the earth with me?"

"Well, I'm not sure about that far." She laughed and tousled his hair. "Now, you're the worrywart."

Her response wasn't what he wanted to hear. Why hadn't she responded with a resounding yes?

He saw a quizzical expression on her face. Then she chuckled. "I think you have the jitters, taking me to meet your mother."

"Maybe that's my problem." He tried to be jovial, but he knew that wasn't his problem at all.

She shook her head at him.

He said no more, but embraced her warm, loving body, and they stood together quietly. Then he pulled himself away, kissing her good-bye. He felt disappointed in himself. He so wanted to tell her what had been pressing on his mind for days, but he couldn't. He feared her reaction and didn't want to ruin her visit to the Cape. He'd wait until the end of her stay.

&

On Friday morning at the Barnstable County Airport on the Cape, Sally came through the gate. Brad waited for her, alone, and she wondered if it were the children's choice or his.

"Hi. How was your flight?" he asked, putting his arm around her and kissing her quickly as they walked through the terminal.

"Not bad at all. By the time they served the coffee and breakfast, I thought we'd land before I finished."

"Alice and Ed drove you to the airport?"

"Yep. They're great. They said they'd keep an eye on the house, plus my garden will look better with Ed in charge than with me keeping it up."

"Mother is planning a welcome luncheon. I hope you didn't fill up too much on that wonderful airplane breakfast."

"No problem. Where are the kids?"

"Oh, Mom convinced them to stay with her and let me pick you up myself."

"I've missed them. I've missed you, too."

His arm encircled her shoulders as they walked to the baggage claim area. When they arrived, the luggage was already circling on the conveyor, and they headed for the car.

The traffic moved steadily along as they headed toward South Dennis. As they turned toward the ocean, they passed through the lovely village of Dennisport situated on Nantucket Sound. Gray and steel-blue clapboard cottages with shuttered windows rose before them on narrow streets. Patches of flower gardens, ragged and wild, tossed in the ocean breeze behind the weathered houses.

Turning down Old Cape Road, Brad announced they were nearly home. Soon the clapboard cottages became sprawling colonial homes on spacious landscaped grounds. Sally gaped, wide-eyed.

"Many of these places were built by wealthy sea captains," Brad said. "Wait until you see our own widow's walk."

"You didn't prepare me for this." She certainly had not contemplated that Brad's mother would live in a mansion.

"Here's our place now." He turned the wheel and the car headed down a tree-lined drive. Sally was astounded.

twelve

Near the end of the driveway an old carriage house stood, covered in white clapboard and sporting window boxes filled with pink and white ivy geraniums and alpine strawberries. At the end of the driveway, a charming three-story colonial house appeared with white clapboards and slate-blue shutters. At the top of the house, Sally saw a small windowed room looking out to the bay with the widow's walk that Brad had mentioned. White and pink hollyhocks, lavender foxglove, and purple yarrow grew in abundance around the wings of the old house.

Her voice caught in her throat, gazing at the splendor of the lovely home. "Brad. It's beautiful."

"Thanks. It is nice, isn't it?" They left the car in the driveway, and Brad opened the trunk to retrieve Sally's luggage. As he lifted it out, children's voices echoed from the entrance.

"Daddy, you're back." Danny came running out of the door toward them. Kelly was close behind. "We made brownies while you were gone."

"Are they still warm? I love warm brownies," Brad said.

"Yep. Sally can have some, too."

"Why, thank you, Danny. I love brownies."

"We're gonna have lunch on the terrace," Kelly announced.

"This is a perfect day for it," Brad said.

As they approached the entrance, Brad's mother appeared at the doorway. She transcended her petite stature by her generous grace and refinement. Her green eyes, the same color as Kelly's, sparkled, and her white hair curled softly around her pleasant face. She stepped forward with her hand extended in greeting.

"Good morning," she said cheerfully. "Welcome to Cape Cod. I hope your flight was pleasant."

Sally stepped forward, taking her hand. "Yes, it was very nice. I'm so happy to be here. What a lovely home you have. And bursting with history, I'm sure."

"Yes. I wish it were our family history, but it is not, you know. Brad's grandfather bought this home, many years ago, from the original family, Captain Jack Slater. It was built in the early nineteenth century."

Brad's mother entered the foyer first, her peach and green print cotton skirt swirling ahead of them, a mint-green cardigan draped from her shoulders. The grand foyer was elegant with its wide, open staircase leading to rooms above.

A parlor on the left connected to the foyer with opened French doors. A dark mahogany fireplace, surrounded by the same dark paneling, lent an air of masculinity to the room. The tall windows looked out to an expanse of rolling green lawn.

On the right, the library housed rows of bookshelves filled with thick volumes and an expansive desk sat to one side. A library table stood on the wall below a large window, affording a view of the stately elms and the carriage house. Two large upholstered chairs were arranged in front of the rugged stone fireplace.

Awestruck, Sally stared at the rooms. Brad headed for the staircase. "Let me carry your bags up to your room."

"Yes. Show Sally her room, Brad," Mrs. Mathews said. Then she turned to Sally. "Take your time. Come down when you are settled, and we will have lunch on the terrace. We are ready when you are."

"Thank you, Mrs. Mathews."

"I will have none of this 'Mrs. Mathews,' my dear. Please, call me Amanda. Mrs. Mathews sounds so stuffy."

"Well then, thank you, Amanda." Sally smiled.

Sally followed Brad up the stairs. The guest room sat in the front of the house, affording a view of Nantucket Bay and the ocean beyond. Sailboats dotted the water, triangles of white against the ever-changing green.

A quilt of dark green and pale lavender print covered the four-poster bed, and a huge armoire stood against one wall. The fireplace and plank flooring covered with large Persian rugs created a cozy feeling.

Brad set her luggage on the bed. "I'm glad you like antiques. The house is loaded with them."

"I love it. Everything's wonderful."

"The kids love it here on the water, and Mother is thrilled to have them."

The children's excited voices echoed outside the windows. Sally looked down and saw the terrace below her window, a large area of stone and cement circled with urns of fuchsia and ivy geraniums. In front of the terrace, roses grew in a patch of garden bordered with colorful Sweet William and clusters of white feverfew. Brad looked out and, catching the eye of the children, waved.

"I'll leave you alone so you can get your things put away. When you're ready, come down, and we'll have lunch."

She walked him to the door where he embraced her and kissed her lovingly. "I'm so glad you're here." He turned and headed back down the staircase.

Sally hung her clothes in the armoire, refreshed her makeup in the bathroom mirror, and ran a comb through her hair. She then returned to the first floor where she knew they were anxiously waiting.

She heard the voices coming from the front of the house as

she reached the bottom of the stairs. She turned toward the open door next to the staircase.

The dining room stood directly in front of her, connected to a vast living room by an open archway. An elegant glass vase held an arrangement of fresh flowers from pink to burgundy—foxglove, yarrow, and delphinium—obviously picked from the flower gardens around the house.

The windows from floor to ceiling looked out to the terrace and the bay beyond. Voices drifted in through the French doors, and Sally caught sight of the children playing on the grass near the water's edge as she stepped onto the sunny terrace.

&

Brad saw Sally immediately as she came through the doorway. Amanda turned, also, and rose from her chair where she and Brad were talking. "Well, you found us," Amanda said. "I hope your room is comfortable."

"Oh, it's wonderful. Every room is beautiful."

"Well, thank you. If you look closely, things are beginning to wear, but it does have charm. Come to the table, and we will eat."

Brad rose as Sally joined them at the patio table beneath a large blue umbrella. He was sipping a tall, frosted glass of iced tea and quickly poured a tumbler for her.

"Children," Amanda called, waving her arm. "Come up to the house. Lunch is ready." She walked back toward the kitchen.

"How does your mother manage this house?"

"She has a day lady, Naomi. She comes in the morning and goes home after dinner. For years we had a couple who lived over the carriage house."

The children's voices drew closer, and by the time Amanda returned from the house, they had reached the table.

"Grandma, there's two big white birds on the water. Are they swans?" Kelly asked, bursting with excitement. "They have long necks."

"Well then, I imagine they are."

Naomi brought a large tray to the table and laid before them a basket of crusty rolls, a plate of sliced fresh vegetables, and crab salad. Leaving, she returned with a bowl piled with fresh fruit and a second frosty pitcher filled with lemonade.

"Thank you, Naomi," Amanda said as the woman headed back to the kitchen. "Brad, would you say the blessing?"

They bowed their heads, and Brad offered thanks for the food and for Sally's safe journey. Without hesitation, they filled their plates. Brad studied his mother's face as she chatted with Sally. If she had any concerns, they didn't show.

Sally seemed relaxed and dished salad for the children, speaking to them as if they were important to the conversation. The children's response filled Brad with pleasure. He had wondered if the day would ever come that he could feel this kind of joy.

Finally Danny burst into the conversation. "Let's take Sally to Chatham and see the fish boats."

Brad chuckled. "You do like to watch the fish boats."

Danny nodded. "I like to watch the fish go down the slide and see the big pile of fish heads."

Amanda grimaced. "Oh dear, Danny, I am not sure fish heads is a good topic for our lunch."

"Danny, you're making us all sick," moaned Kelly.

Brad, trying not to smile, spoke to Danny. "Okay. No more fish talk until after lunch, either of you. I promise we'll take Sally to Chatham. If nothing more, she'll enjoy the Chatham Light."

Later that afternoon, they followed the highway to Chatham. The ride took them through little fishing villages nestled along the bay. They headed first for the Chatham pier to watch the fishing boats come in, bringing their catches for the day. Vessel after vessel pulled up to the fish chute, emptying their cleaned, headless catch to be weighed. Seagulls wheeled overhead, landing on the pier and soaring off again, confiscating a tasty morsel for themselves.

Danny clapped his hands as the fish slid down the chute, pointing as he saw the great container of fish heads sitting on the boat deck. Kelly claimed it was disgusting, but her glowing face attested that she enjoyed the excitement, too. Leaving the pier, they drove to the lighthouse itself, standing tall over the vast sandy beach stretching out on the peninsula below. The sun glowed behind the towering building, creating a vibrant silhouette.

"Tomorrow we can drive up to Provincetown. You'll see some great lighthouses on the way. Some of the oldest on the Cape."

"Let's take our bathing suits," Kelly said. "Sally wants to swim, don't you?"

Her expression hungered for a positive answer, and Sally didn't disappoint her. Brad wanted to hug her in front of them all.

"Swimming it will be," Brad said. "There are good beaches along the way." He chuckled at his own excitement. "Sally Newgate, we'll certainly show you the whole Cape in the week you're here." Then he remembered, and he knew he would show her more than the Cape. He prayed she would be thrilled.

❧

That night Sally slept well, and in the morning, she awoke relaxed and ready for the day. Her window opened onto the bay, and she could hear the sound of waves crashing on the shore and the call of the seagulls. A breeze blew in through the window, and the thin curtains billowed and fell with its motion. Hearing no sounds from below, she showered and dressed quickly and quietly, not wanting to wake the others.

To her surprise as she entered the breakfast room, the whole family was seated around the breakfast table.

As she entered, Danny's voice boomed. "Good, now we don't have to be quiet. Daddy said we had to be quiet until you got up."

"He did?" Sally chuckled. "You must have done a good job. I thought everyone was still in bed and I was the first one up."

"We surprised you then, didn't we?" Brad winked. "You look bright and chipper."

"Did you sleep well, Sally?" Amanda asked.

"Oh, very well, thanks. The sound of the waves on the beach is like a lullaby."

"Good, I am pleased. Now, help yourself, there, on the buffet. Naomi has made a lovely breakfast for us."

Sally ate her fill, and after breakfast, they set out on their trip to Provincetown. At the Coast Guard Beach in Eastham the frothy waves rolled in from the ocean, and Brad parked the car. When they unloaded their gear, they trudged to the beach.

The water was cold coming in from the ocean, and the children chose to play in the sand and walk the water's edge rather than swim. Brad and Sally swam near the shore, wanting to be close to the youngsters.

Back on the hot sand, they lay on blankets, feeling the warm sun on their backs, the ocean breeze offering a false sense of coolness.

"You know, I think I'm getting a sunburn," Sally said, pulling on her top. "We'd better check the children."

She rose and walked to where the children were playing in

the sand. "Are you starting to sunburn?" She reached down and touched Danny's shoulders. "How about you, Kelly?" she asked.

Kelly, engrossed in her sand castle, didn't look up. "No, Mommy, I'm not sunburned." As the words left her mouth, a look of confusion and embarrassment covered Kelly's face. Sally knelt in the sand to comfort her, but the child jumped up, tears streaming down her cheeks, and ran toward Brad, throwing herself into his arms.

"What happened, sweetheart?" He hadn't heard her mistake. She didn't speak, but buried her face in his shoulder. Brad looked questioningly at Sally. She didn't want to embarrass Kelly any more by telling him what happened.

Danny hurried to his father and provided the details. "Kelly called Sally *mommy*. Wasn't that silly? She's not our mommy." Then he leaned over, looking into Kelly's face. "Why are you crying, Kelly?" He patted her shoulder. "It's okay."

Brad looked helplessly at the children.

Sally also didn't know what to do. She picked up Kelly's blouse and handed it to Brad. "Here's Kelly's blouse. I do think they're getting a little sunburned." Then she turned to Danny. "Let's put this shirt on, or you'll look like a lobster and people will try to have you for dinner."

Danny giggled, oblivious to the tension around him. Brad helped Kelly into her blouse.

Sally took Danny by the hand and wandered down the beach, chattering about the seagulls and the sand castle.

"Why did Kelly call you 'mommy'?" Danny asked as they splashed through the water's edge.

"She made a mistake, Danny. She was so busy with her sand castle, I think she got mixed up. She'll be fine." Sally squeezed his hand, and they continued down the beach. Later

Brad and Kelly joined them, and the four strolled along the shore, feet dragging through the foamy water. They walked until they saw the Nauset Light with its bright red roof on the rocky slopes above them. Nothing more was said about Kelly's slip of the tongue.

thirteen

Sunday morning they piled into Amanda's station wagon and headed for Beautiful Savior Church to attend worship service. When they arrived, Brad stood with Sally outside the typical picture-postcard New England church as she admired its wide white planks and a tall spire rising high into the sky.

The belfry housed a great iron bell, and as they entered the church, the bell ended its deep resonant toll and the small pipe organ sounded, filling the air with its sweet tones. Amanda glowed as she nodded to her friends and acquaintances, especially when she introduced Sally to some of her closer friends. Amanda obviously hoped Brad had found a new wife and mother for the children.

That evening Naomi stayed with the children, and the three adults drove into Chatham to the Old Chatham Inn where they enjoyed dinner in an elegant eighteenth-century captain's mansion overlooking the bay where sailboats glided along the dark green waters, leaving white foamy trails in their wake.

Amanda's warm feelings toward Sally pleased Brad. After talking over the menu choices, they gave their orders to the waitress. She returned shortly with bowls of chowder, thick with clams. By the time they had eaten the salad, they only nibbled at the entrees now in front of them.

Amanda stared out toward the sea. Low in the sky, the sun spread its palette of warm colors across the darkening water. "Do you remember when we came here a couple of years ago?"

Her question jolted Brad. "Sure, we've eaten here many times."

"Janet sat where Sally is sitting. I remember the sunlight streaking through her hair like gold and red flames. Her hair was very beautiful."

Discomfort shifted through him, and he glanced at Sally as she squirmed in her seat. She avoided looking directly at Amanda or Brad.

"Janet's hair was beautiful, Mom. Why would you mention that?"

"Seeing the sunlight glinting in such fiery colors on the water, I suppose. I look at the children and feel so badly for them sometimes."

"They're adjusting, Mother. It takes time. They've made progress."

She lowered her eyes. "Yes, I suppose they have."

Brad gazed at Sally, hoping she accepted his silent apology. "Let's talk about something else."

Amanda looked up, her eyes widening. "I am sorry. I didn't mean to offend you, Sally."

Sally placed her hand on Amanda's. "You don't need to apologize. I understand loss. I've gone through more than two years of it myself. It's not fun. Brad's right, though. The children have made real strides since I first met them. They'll be fine." Sally patted her hand and placed hers back in her lap.

Amanda sat in silence and then changed the subject as quickly as she had mentioned Janet. "What do you have planned for tomorrow?"

Brad felt a mixture of irritation and sorrow, sadness for his mother's pain but anger that she had brought this up in front of Sally. "Would you like to join us ferrying over to Martha's Vineyard?"

Amanda lifted her sad eyes to his, her apology evident.

"Yes, I would like that. Perhaps we could have dinner on the island."

When they arrived home, Sally and Brad sat on the terrace alone. "Sally, I'm sorry about my mother today—bringing up Janet. I don't believe she meant to hurt you or compare you to Janet."

"I know that, Brad. You and the kids live with your loss day in and day out. Your mother only sees it when you visit. She can push it out of her mind in her day-to-day life, but when she's with you, the emptiness clangs in her head like a buoy out on Nantucket Sound. She needs more time to adjust. She's hurting for the children—and for you."

He looked into her eyes. "Thanks for understanding." He rose. "How about a walk?" He offered Sally his hand, and she clasped it. They walked to the darkened beach. The sky shimmered with stars and a crescent moon reflected on the waves rolling onto the shore. They looked silently across the water.

Brad thought about the past days, about Kelly's error calling Sally "mommy" and Sally's gentle message to his mother. The time together knitted them like a family—joy, sorrow, frustration, and love. He pushed his fears aside. *She'll accept my proposal,* he thought. *She must.*

☙

Sally felt as eager as the children when they climbed into the car the next morning to go to Falmouth for their trip to Martha's Vineyard. But she felt frustration, too, wishing she and Brad had more time alone together. She sensed Brad had thoughts he wanted to share with her, but time and proximity hadn't worked well in their favor. In the few minutes they had alone, a deep conversation didn't seem appropriate.

At the pier, when the great doors of the ferry opened, they drove onto the lower deck, and leaving the station wagon, they made their way to the upper decks for their departure.

The children begged to be on the top deck where they could sit outside in the sun and feel the ocean breeze. But when they reached the open water, the air felt too chilly for Amanda, so she and Sally returned to a closed cabin where they had their first opportunity to talk privately.

"Sally, I want to apologize for my reminiscence yesterday. It was terribly rude of me to speaking of Janet in front of you."

"Not at all, Amanda. Janet was very much a part of your life. We can't forget people we love."

"Janet's loss was terrible, certainly. She was a fine daughter-in-law, but that's not my grief, really. The children need a mother, and Brad needs a wife."

Sally's chest tightened, and her stomach knotted. "Yes, that's true."

"I am so pleased that Brad asked you to come for a visit. I am sure you are aware how much you mean to him."

Sally opened her mouth to speak, but Amanda continued.

"It broke my heart to see him in such pain, and the little ones were like tiny boats tossed on the wind—so insecure and frightened. You have been good for all of them, Sally."

Sally looked into the older woman's sincere face. *Is this what she was getting at?* Sally's thoughts had rumbled in her mind earlier, thinking perhaps Amanda disliked her. "Brad and the children have been good for me, too. I thought I was doing okay, and then, little things threw me off kilter. When I became ill after Tim died, I finally agreed to attend a grief recovery program. That's where I met Brad, you know. I thank God for having met him."

"I want you to know how much I have enjoyed your being here. I do not want to interfere in your relationship. I loved Janet. She was a wonderful wife and mother, but she is gone. I do not want the children to be without a mother—nor Brad, for that matter, to be without a wife who loves him. I believe you do love my son. Please forgive me if I am out of place. We have not been alone so that I could tell you these things."

"Yes, I know," Sally said gently. "Brad and I care very much for each other. We both have dealt with terrible changes in our lives—losing our mates. The children have had a difficult time, too. And you're right. Brad and the children mean a great deal to me."

Amanda took Sally's hand in hers. "They mean 'a great deal' to you, but do you *love* them? Watching all of you, I think you do. I pray you love them. I do not want to see them hurt. You seem like a wonderful woman, and whatever feelings you have, I thank you for all you have done for my son and my grandchildren. They are smiling again, and they did not do that for a long time."

"I'm smiling again, too. They've done that for me."

As she finished her sentence, the children came bounding forward with Brad in their wake. They were oblivious to the conversation they interrupted, but Brad, with knowing eyes, saw Sally's hand in Amanda's and knew they had been talking.

"Daddy said we could have lunch in the snack bar," Kelly said. "Would you like something?"

"Certainly, we would," Amanda agreed, and they rose to find the snack bar.

Sally looked at the family—now seeming like family of her own—and a myriad of emotions bubbled inside her. The time they had spent together seemed to be a mixture of beautiful moments interrupted by exuberant children. She would have loved each second, except for a gripping fear that clung to her thoughts.

❧

Brad watched the days pass quickly—too quickly. The thought of Sally leaving left a rift in his life. He longed to keep her by his side. In the middle of the week, he took the entire family on a ride to Providence, Rhode Island—an hour and a half drive. They questioned his sanity, but he didn't respond. He had his reason, but he wanted to wait and share the lovely town with them first before he told them everything.

They drove through the city, passing the bustling business area and admired the restored eighteenth-century mansions winding through the old city.

When they visited the Roger Williams Park, the children scampered from the car, eager to get their legs free from the confines of the backseat. They had sat patiently for the long ride, Amanda between them.

"A zoo, Daddy." Danny pointed ahead, and they followed behind the children.

The animals provided their usual antics, producing delighted giggles from the children. Amanda hugged Danny and Kelly periodically, and Sally watched her with a smile of approval. As the children skipped off toward the monkeys, Amanda held back and waited for Brad and Sally to catch up.

"This is pleasant, Brad, but I do not understand why we came here. It is a long drive to look at monkeys and old buildings."

"I thought you'd enjoy the day, Mother. It's different, isn't it—and a charming city."

"Obviously, I cannot deny that, but I am still confused."

Sally added her floundering thoughts. "I've wondered myself, Brad. The Cape has so many lovely places, I'm not sure why we're here."

"You two," he said, trying to cover his ruse. "Can't a guy take his two favorite women and children to see a nice city?" He had done his best to show them everything he could in the area.

They shook their heads, but didn't ask any more questions.

When Brad woke on Friday, he felt restless. Not only was it Sally's last full day on the Cape, but last night he had rehearsed in his mind the thoughts that had been tossing in his brain since before she arrived. Tonight had to be the night for his confession.

Brad wandered down for breakfast, knowing he had to face the day with a smile. The children and Amanda were nearly finished, and when Sally entered the breakfast room, he sat alone waiting for her and reading the morning paper.

Sally stood in the doorway, her face glowing as she looked at him. "Where is everyone? Is this the first morning I beat the rest out of bed?"

Brad regarded her with a smile. "Sorry. You lose. Mom and the kids are out in the yard."

"I don't understand why I sleep so soundly here. It's embarrassing." She wandered to the buffet and poured a cup of fragrant coffee.

"It shouldn't be. It means you're relaxed and enjoying yourself. I take it as a compliment."

Sally carried the cup to the breakfast table. "Well, good, I hope your mother does. She might think I'm lazy."

"I doubt that, but then, what if she does? Perhaps it's the truth." He grinned at her over the top of his newspaper.

Sally grabbed the napkin from her place setting and threw it at Brad. He ducked, and it sailed over his head as Amanda entered the room. "Well, am I walking in on a quarrel? I think not, since you are both smiling."

Sally grinned and returned to the buffet. "Your son is taunting me—he said I was lazy, which we all know is not true." Sally filled her plate with apple pancakes and a patty of breakfast sausage and carried the contents to the table. "Plus, this coffee is wonderful, and don't tell me—it's something cream. . .aha, vanilla cream. Am I right?"

"Yes, indeed, and anyone with such keen taste buds cannot be lazy, as my son has suggested."

Brad faked a pout. "Oh, fine. Gang up on me. I can take it. And my own mother, too!"

"Take what, Daddy? Take what?" Kelly asked as she twirled into the room, carrying a plastic bucket overflowing with flowers from the garden.

"I need help, Kelly. Your Grandma and Sally are ganging up on me. Protect me."

"I can't Daddy, 'cuz I'm one of the girls, you know. We girls stick together."

Brad threw his hands over his face in a dramatic gesture of defeat. They laughed and applauded. Brad, enjoying the levity, rose and took a deep bow. Danny darted into the room, apparently thinking he missed something. Brad grabbed him under the arms, swung him up in the air, then brought him to his chest. "My only real friend. Right here." He gave Danny a loud, smacking kiss. Danny giggled and squirmed until Brad set him down.

"Do that to me, Daddy." Kelly giggled and, setting the bucket on the floor, jumped up and down in front of him. Brad knew it was impossible to play with one and not include the other, so he picked her up and repeated the motions until she too laughed and wriggled to be released. "Before I let you go, Mary Quite Contrary, where did you get those flowers?" He nodded toward the bouquet of flowers jutting from the bucket where she set it.

"Grandma and I picked them. Aren't they pretty?" She bent down and retrieved the container, showing them to Brad. "We're going to put them in a vase for the living room. But I have a special one for Sally." She reached into the bucket and, moving the flowers around, brought out a perfect rose, delicate pink fading to white edges.

fourteen

Kelly handed Sally the lovely rose. Sally looked down at the slim blond girl beaming up at her, and tears gathered on the rim of her eyes. She reached down, taking the rose and gained time to control herself by taking a deep smell of its fragrance. Then she knelt and kissed Kelly's soft, cool cheek.

"Thank you, my princess." Sally's voice was a whisper, barely audible. Kelly reached around her shoulders and hugged her.

Amanda, realizing it was an extraordinary occasion, broke the solemn silence with an air of business. "We had better get those flowers in water, Kelly. Flowers need water to stay fresh and lovely. Come with me, and I will give you a bud vase for Sally's rose." Kelly followed her grandmother through the door with Danny running behind them.

Sally was grateful for the intrusion. Brad gazed at Sally in amazement. "And we were worried." His voice, too, broke with emotion. He walked to Sally, taking his handkerchief from his pocket and wiping the tears which were still clinging to her lashes. She lay her head on his shoulder for a moment, allowing herself to savor the precious memory of Kelly's gift. She stepped back, her eyes drinking in his joy. "You have wonderful children, Mr. Mathews."

Later in the day, as Sally dressed for evening, she gazed at the delicate rose in the crystal bud vase. She thought again about the week she had spent with Brad's loving family, and she bowed her head, thanking God for the gift.

Dinner and a performance at the Cape Playhouse was

Brad's special treat for her. Since her arrival, this was the first evening they'd shared alone. Not too distant from the Cape Playhouse, they ate in Yarmouthport at the Old Colonial House Inn where she delighted in a meal of baked fish stuffed with lobster, crabmeat, and scallops. The play proved to be amusing. The entire evening was a memorable ending to a special week.

When they left the playhouse, the moon glowed, bright and clear, and a soft, warm breeze gently stirred the leaves. Instead of heading back to Dennisport, Brad turned down Beach Street to a quiet stretch of sandy shore. He pulled the car off the road, and opening Sally's door, he helped her out. A salty breeze drifted in from the bay, ruffling her hair against her cheek. Brad took her hand in his as they walked to the sand.

A large boulder protruded from the ground. They sat against its rough surface and looked out at the dark waters of Cape Cod Bay. Brad held her hand in his and caressed it gently, in silence. Sensing they had come here for a reason, Sally waited nervously.

Brad finally spoke. "You know that I want to talk to you, and I don't know quite where to begin. I have so much to say."

Sally's hands became clammy, and her legs trembled against the stone. Though the week had seemed so perfect, full of love and companionship, something foreboding had hung on the air. An icy fear streaked through her.

❧

Brad had sensed Sally's nervousness all evening. She sat against the rock, her hands folded like a knot resting against her lap. His own heart pounded within his chest so loudly he thought she might hear it. "First, I want to tell you that I love you. I have no question, no doubt. I love you with all that I have. I've prayed and asked for guidance, and I believe this is good."

Sally touched his arm. "What, Brad?"

He shook his head. "I know we haven't known each other for very long, although it seems to me it's been forever. Time isn't important when you find someone who shares your faith, your interests, and your love."

"Brad—"

"Please, Sally, let me have my say. I have it memorized." He smiled, hoping to see a smile in return.

A faint grin appeared on her lips.

"I know that you love the kids, and that's very important to me. Most of all, I believe you love me as I love you. We've said all along that we have plenty of time to get to know each other and assure ourselves that our feelings are real. We said there's no rush."

He paused and looked into her eyes, seeing her concern. "That's where I'm adding a complication."

He heard Sally catch her breath. The time had arrived to say what he had to say. He stood up and walked away from the rock and turned back to her and knelt in the sand. "I've been offered a promotion. I say *offered,* but it's more like a command. If I turn this down, it will end my chances to advance in the company, and I can't do that to the kids, to myself, and God willing, to you."

In the moonlight, Brad saw Sally's face register confusion. He took her tightly knotted hands in his. "The promotion means that I have to leave Michigan. Our sightseeing trip to Providence had an ulterior motive behind it. The corporation has a branch office there, and that's where my promotion will take me. It has its advantages, besides the expected raise in salary and position in the company."

What he feared, Brad saw now in Sally's face. Confusion,

anxiety, panic. But he had to go on. "It brings us closer to my mom who, despite her good health, is getting older. She loves the children and misses them, and we miss her. She'll never leave her home on the Cape, and I'd never ask her to move. Living in Providence means that we can see her more often."

Brad raised Sally's hand and kissed her cold fingers. "I am asking you to come here with me—marry me, and we can make a new home together."

Brad held his breath, his gaze riveted to hers. Moving, he thought, would solve some of the problems. Sally and he would have a new home, one without old memories. They could start anew and fresh; her, not sitting in Janet's chair at the table and him, not hanging his clothes in Tim's closet.

Sally gazed at him, still on his knees in the damp sand. She raised her hand to her chest and closed her eyes. "Oh, Brad, we said we had time. . ." When she opened them, Brad saw tears mist her lashes, then run down her cheeks, dripping on his hands as they held hers.

He rose, and wrapped his arm around her. He felt her tremble against him and his own sudden fear joined hers. "I showed you the beauty of this area and a little of Providence. I know it means giving up your job, but there are many jobs in Providence, and Sally, I want us to have a baby—our own little boy or girl. Kelly and Danny would love it, I know."

She opened her mouth to speak, but he silenced her. "Please don't answer me now, Sally. You need time to make your decision, I know." He placed his cheek against hers and pressed her close. "I know we thought we had all the time in the world, but the situation makes it different. That's why I wanted you to think about this while I'm here on the Cape.

"I haven't told Mom or the kids about the move yet. I wanted to talk to you first. When I get back to Michigan, I'll put my house up for sale. I have to be in Providence by the first of September. It'll work out best for the children because they can start their new school at the beginning of the school year. It doesn't give us much time, I know."

She hadn't spoken but clung to him. He placed his lips on hers and tasted the salt from her tears. He felt her mouth yield to his and his kiss deepened, his desire for her crying with a silent voice into the night sky. When their emotions were drained, he unwrapped his arms from around her, and they walked in silence through the sand to the car.

≷≋

Sally awoke with a headache and was very tired. She had lain awake much of the night, thinking about Brad's proposal. Instinctively, she wanted to say "yes, yes, yes." Though fears and concerns prodded her *yes* to *I don't know* to *I am afraid*. She felt a horrible pressure in her chest. All the words of caution filled her—Elaine, Darby, Bill, and Sue. The truth was they had known each other less than a year. She remembered other couples she knew—like Cassie who thought she was in love—whose marriage ended so quickly. Christian marriage was "until death," and she couldn't make a mistake.

With Brad, her life seemed joyful, but she wanted their relationship to be right. Questions circled through her mind. Was she ready for a new husband? Did she have the courage to leave Michigan? To leave her friends, family, Carrie? Her whole life was there.

Sally sat in frozen silence on the edge of her bed, looking at her half-packed suitcase. Her world spun in her head. How could she answer his question? She loved him. This week validated and assured her that she loved him and the children, but was it a love that would last? Was it what God wanted for her? And moving? Could she do that? Tears rolled from her eyes. Yet, how could she say good-bye to them?

Then her thoughts soared back to Jack Holbrook's talks. Love is not spread out or divided. It grows. Why did she fear this love that lived in her heart? She knew Brad loved her. The kids were growing to love her. Amanda liked her. Then why was she so afraid? She rose and stared outside, the thoughts stirring in her mind—tossing to and fro like the rhythm of the waves lapping the shore outside her window.

She forced herself to confront the day. In the mirror, her face looked tired, creased with lack of sleep, eyes streaked with red. Even after showering and putting on lipstick and blush, she looked pale and tense. In a hotel, she would have called room service, but here she was forced to descend the stairs for breakfast and appear normal. She did not feel normal.

❧

Amanda and Brad were alone in the breakfast room when Sally entered. Brad was startled by Sally's expression, and his hopes fell.

Amanda's face registered a look of concern. "Sally, I hope you are not ill. Did you sleep poorly?"

"Yes, I'm afraid so." Sally attempted to sound casual.

"That is just the way it is. Whenever I travel, the night before I leave for my trip and the night before I return home, I lie awake much of the night. It is very irritating."

"Oh, I'll be fine after some coffee."

Brad listened to the conversation, observing Sally cover her distress. He watched her in disbelief. Though he realized the possibility, he had thought his proposal would be received with joy, not grief. He knew the move to Providence might seem difficult, but wouldn't it solve so many problems? That's what he had thought. Apparently he was utterly wrong. "I'm sorry you didn't rest well. Tonight, you'll be home in your own bed. Maybe you can sleep in tomorrow." He knew better, but he had to say something.

"I'm fine, Brad. Thanks."

Sally filled a cup with coffee, glancing at the choices on the buffet table, and then sat down without taking anything. Amanda observed the tension and rose from her seat. "I had better check on the children. Will you excuse me?" Before anyone could reply, she left the room.

"Sally, my proposal last night has upset you. I'm so sorry. I didn't mean to end our wonderful week on such a bad note."

"Please, Brad. It's not a bad note—confusing, scary maybe— but not bad. It's me and my crazy mind. Thoughts jumped back and forth, up and down, and I couldn't get them to rest. I've many things to think about, and I want to think with a clear, rational mind. I want my answer to be the best for all of us."

"I know, Sally, but don't be too rational. Let your heart speak, too."

"Oh, my heart has spoken, Brad. I love you. But marriage means so many changes. I don't know how many changes I can handle. And do we really know each other well enough? Marriage is for a lifetime. Please be patient with me." *A lifetime*. Her thoughts drifted back to her few years with Tim.

"I'll be patient—as patient as I can be, anyway." He smiled and placed his hand on hers, moving his thumb across the softness of her skin.

Loud footsteps tromped in the hall, and both children burst into the room, squealing. Brad released Sally's hand.

"Kelly found a frog by the water. She said she was going to teach it things and put it on a leash, Daddy." Danny's eyes sparkled with delight.

"Frogs might make good pets," Kelly pleaded. "They're quiet, Daddy."

"Not real quiet. They spend the night croaking. I think we'll leave the frog here with Grandma. You can visit it when you come again."

Kelly's lower lip dropped to a pout.

"Sally, we're going to the airport with you and see your plane fly," Danny chattered. "You can look down from the sky, and I'll be waving at you."

"That'll be nice, Danny. You probably won't be able to see me, but I'll be waving back."

Brad had forgotten his promise to the kids. He and Sally needed to talk. But when? "I told them when you arrived that if they stayed home with Grandma, I'd let them take you back to the airport. Leave it to them to remember."

"That's fine," Sally said softly.

"Aren't you hungry?" Kelly asked, noticing Sally's empty place mat. "Are you sad to go home? You look sad."

"I am sad to be leaving all of you, but adults have to go to work. In fact, I need to get the rest of my things together, or I'll miss my flight." She rose and took a step toward the door, then paused. "It won't take me a minute." She continued down the hall and up the stairway.

Amanda didn't join them at the airport. They said their good-byes outside the lovely old house. Sally took Amanda's hand, but to her surprise, Amanda leaned over and kissed her cheek. Sally returned the kiss.

The children were excited at the airport, pressing their noses against the observation windows and watching the planes pull into the gates. When it was time to board, they each gave her a big hug and to her surprise, a kiss. She was moved by their genuine, simple affection, and felt her eyes brim with tears. She quickly wiped away the tears with the back of her hand without being obvious, at least to the children.

The children looked at Brad. "Say good-bye, Daddy," Kelly said, watching his every move. Sally's heart lurched, wondering how he would respond. Then, she knew. He stepped forward and embraced Sally as the children had done, then kissed her quickly and gently on the lips. When their gaze returned to the children, Kelly and Danny looked at them with nothing more than a loving smile on their excited faces. At that moment, joy swept over her, despite her strained departure.

"I'll call you tonight," Brad said, as she started down the ramp to the plane. She nodded. The children waved, and she turned and waved back at them before rounding the corner. When she was out of sight she allowed her tears to flow freely down her cheeks.

&

On the plane, Sally closed her eyes and thought, holding back her tears. After Tim's death, she knew her life had ended, but little by little, she had carved a new life out of the rock of despair and sadness. Then she met Brad. New joy blossomed in her life, but with her joy came new heartaches, Kelly's unhappiness, and the concerned comments from family and friends.

For so long, she had prayed for God to guide her, and she'd been angry when no answer came, nothing to give her a sense of God's will. Now, a new life was hers for the taking. Brad and the kids loved her, and he offered her a new beginning.

So why was she clinging to the past? Her house, her job, family, friends, and her familiar world? Her faith had been so strong after Tim died. Through those hard times, she felt God's hand guiding her along. But then time went on and she waited. She waited for God to give her the promised time under heaven, her season. *Is this it, Lord? Tell me? I've known Brad less than a year. Do I leave all I've ever known with the hope I'm following Your will? Lord, I'm waiting to hear Your voice.*

When Sally arrived home, she walked through the lonely rooms, then sat with her face in her hands and wept. That night she dreamed. She was there on the Cape with them all, watching whales leap into the sky and dive deep into the vast unknown of the dark blue waters.

❧

When Brad returned from the Cape, his stress was evident. He had the difficult task of putting his home up for sale and packing his belongings. His firm assisted in the move by locating homes fitting his needs. All he needed to do was fly to Providence and make a decision. Within three days, he placed a bid on a house in an excellent location with an elementary school only two blocks away.

Sally was grateful he didn't push for an answer. He waited. But September was at hand, and his move was imminent. Two weeks before he moved, Sally invited Brad for a quiet evening at home. After dinner, she sat next to him on the mauve and gray living room sofa and gave him her answer.

fifteen

"I can't marry you, Brad." Tears ran down her cheeks and dripped on her hands knotted in her lap.

Brad's heart fell—his world fell at his feet. The fears that had filled him were now a horrible reality. He took her soft, cold hand in his and listened.

"I've prayed. I need time. I don't know why you're so certain, and I'm not. I know I love you, but I'm. . .I wish I could sell this house and throw my arms around you and walk away to a new place and a new life, but I can't—not now." Her downcast eyelids raised, tears clinging to her lashes. "Yet, I can't say good-bye."

Brad opened his mouth and heard his husky, unsure voice. "I suppose I expected you to tell me this. I prayed that you wouldn't. I don't want you to marry me unless you know it's right for you. I want to share my life with you—forever. I want to share Kelly and Danny with you, and I want to have a child with you. But most of all, I want you to want that too, and until you do, I'll have to wait and pray."

He paused, fighting back the tears that stung his eyes. "I can't stand being without you. The last two weeks on the Cape were horrible because I knew you left confused and uncertain. I can't tell you the happiness I felt when you were there. I don't know how we'll manage without you." He slid his arms around her, wanting to bury his face in her neck and sob. His body trembled as wildly as hers.

"Brad, I know. Life's wonderful when I'm with you, and I missed you the weeks you were away. I don't know what I'll do when you're really gone."

Suddenly his despair turned to anger. He sat clinging to her, his mind screaming out his love, but she couldn't offer the same. She doubted her own feelings. He couldn't comprehend her fears. "You've answered my question. Let's not dwell on it. I'm leaving in a couple of weeks, and I'd like our last days to be pleasant memories." Sarcasm and irony sizzled in his voice.

❧

Brad dragged through the week, struggling with the loose ends on his job and working late hours. His last days with Sally exhibited feeble attempts at lightheartedness. They lived a lie. Their last dinner together lay in a lump at the bottom of his stomach. His body knotted with tension, and his best attempts at acting were a failure.

Sally's lips trembled as she spoke. "Brad, you and I met at a very difficult time for both of us. We were hurting, both of us reaching out to have questions answered. We needed support. We needed people who understood our loneliness and our grief. You needed someone to help you pull the children through their sorrow. We've been there for each other, and I guess that's why we met."

Astounded, he gaped at her. "That's how it began, Sally. We needed support, and we got it from a lot of people, including each other. So, what does this mean?"

"It means that's why God brought us together. Maybe that's all our meeting was meant to be. I wonder if your move is God's way of telling us to let go, to get on with our lives, wherever that leads us. You should be free to find someone to be a mother for Kelly and Danny—someone to love." Tears edged their way down her cheek and dripped from her chin, but she sat staunch and erect.

The anger he'd pushed below the surface tore through him. Heat rose to his face, and his hands balled into tight fists.

"What are you saying? Have you found someone else? Is this your way of telling me?"

She shook her head, her voice quivering without control. "No, Brad, I have no one but you."

He rose, towering over her. "Then are you telling me that God doesn't want us to love each other? How can you say that, Sally? How can you sit there with tears pouring from your eyes and tell me you don't love me?"

"I'm not saying I don't love you." She swallowed, and a sob tore from her throat. "I've prayed and prayed, Brad, but I can't seem to let go of my life here. You and the kids have become a huge part of it, but I've asked God to give me strength—to give me an answer. I don't feel it, and I don't hear it. I think God's silence is the answer. It's over."

His body quivered uncontrollably, and the words shot from him. "Over! I thought you were a sane, rational, loving woman, but tonight, you've gone mad. Do you think that I can turn off my feelings for you by your words, 'It's over'? You tear my heart out suggesting such a thing. Are you waiting for trumpets and a fanfare from God? What are you expecting for an answer? Can't you listen to your heart? Doesn't your heart speak of love and happiness with us?"

He paced in front of her, his fist pounding in the palm of his hand, his heart pounding as loudly in his chest. "You've certainly fooled me, Sally, if this were a practice session for getting on with your life; I'm not practicing. I'm *loving* you—here and now. You can go ahead and forget about us if you can, but I'm not forgetting about you. I'll pray God brings you to your senses."

He swung to face her. She sat frozen to the sofa cushion, unmoving, tears dripping to her skirt. His dreams crashed around him. He turned and bolted from the room, and for all he knew, from her life.

❧

Following Brad's move, the weeks dragged by. Sally filled her days, but nothing had meaning. Each time the telephone rang, she jumped, her nerves like frayed edges of a hem trailing noticeably behind her. Beth's call from Los Angeles saying she had returned from her hiatus in Africa brought with it sad news of Esther Newgate's steady decline. Work was her only reprieve, distracting her from all that mattered.

Elaine, near the end of her pregnancy, called, and her apology hung in Sally's mind. "Don't let the thoughtless, irrational words I blurted months ago make you doubt Brad and the love you share. This could be a match made in Heaven."

A match made in Heaven. That's what she wanted to hear from God, not Elaine. But she'd told Brad to go, and their parting had left only hurt and anger.

❧

The third week in September, Jim Davidson purchased a block of tickets for the Renaissance Festival held in the rural town of Holly. The activity took the place of their annual company picnic. Sally was in no mood to attend, but Darby and others prodded her to go. Finally, she agreed, but her heart wasn't in it.

She wandered with Darby and Eric through the milling, boisterous crowds in the fifteenth-century setting, listening to minstrels play on their lutes and recorders and hearing the sweet sounds of dulcimers echo on the breeze.

After their picnic lunch, Darby halted in front of some bales of hay formed into a large circle. "Looks like the Renaissance Players are doing a skit. Want to stop?"

"Sure," Eric said, glancing at Sally.

The thought of a lighthearted play left Sally cold. Darby and Eric had welcomed her along, but she felt like an extra shoe, and she needed to get away. "If you don't mind, I think

I'll take a walk back to the vendor stalls. I'd like to get one of those elfin dolls for Carrie—remember those cute gnome characters?"

Darby paused. "We pass that stall again when we leave, don't we?"

But Eric answered the question, "No. I think it's in the other direction."

Darby shrugged. "I guess you're right." She squeezed Sally's arm. "We'll wait here for you, okay?"

Sally agreed, and following the festival map, she headed toward the vendors' booths. Along the way, she was cut off by a parade of the King and Queen and their court, and as she waited, she felt a hand rub across her back. She swung around and gaped into Steve's grinning face. She tensed. Earlier, she'd seen him watching her, but she ignored him, and he left her alone.

"What's a lovely young woman like you doing wandering alone?" The words slid from his lips.

She stepped forward, and his hand dropped from her back. "I'm heading back to the huts." She nodded in the direction of the vendors' stalls. The parade passed by, and she continued toward her destination with Steve on her heels.

"Maybe I'll follow along and see if there's anything I'd like to pick up before I leave." Steve smirked as he moved into step with her.

She ignored him and hurried ahead. The stall she sought was located down a narrow walkway behind a row of thatched huts. She darted through the area that opened to the sun and crowds of people. She glanced behind her, relieved that Steve had stopped to talk to one of the vendors. She kept moving, hoping she'd lost him.

When she located the stall, she examined the delightful, gnarled faces of the dolls and selected one for Carrie. *Why not get one for Kelly? I'll find something for Danny and mail them.* Loneliness tore through her, and she swallowed her sorrow.

She selected another doll, and with her package in hand, she turned and began the trek back toward the picnic area. Stepping into the narrow stretch between the stalls, she heard footsteps behind her. Sharp fear shot through her and she swung around as Steve grabbed her arm, jerking her toward him. "Well, now, I finally have you all to myself."

She struggled to free herself, but he held her pinned against a stall. His hot perfumy breath swept over her face. Screaming seemed foolish. He wasn't a stranger. "Quit playing games, Steve." Her stern voice feigned confidence. "Let go of me. I've had enough of your silliness."

He forced her back like a prisoner. "Silliness? You think I'm playing games? That's what you're playing. You're lonely, and here I am."

His mouth pressed roughly against hers. She could taste the strange scent. She jerked her arm forward and heard her sleeve tear. Quickly she jammed her head upward, bumping his mouth, and a trickle of blood ran down his chin.

He jerked away. "Why, you spitfire," he said.

"Take your hands off me! Don't touch me again!" Her voice resounded in the enclosed area. A hut door banged open, and a young man rushed out to help her.

"Take your hands off the lady!" The young man bellowed, rushing toward him. Others heard his angry voice. More people rounded the corner, and Sally pulled from his grasp, holding her torn sleeve with her hand. She'd dropped the package of dolls and reached down to snatch them from the ground. As the young man confronted Steve, she maneuvered through the crowd and, on shaking legs, hurried back to the picnic area.

৯

The next couple of days at Davidson's were tense. Sally looked for Steve around every corner, in the workroom, and lunchroom, everywhere she went in the building. Then one morning Jim Davidson called her into his office. She went apprehensively.

When she entered, he sat behind his massive walnut desk. As the secretary closed the door, to Sally's surprise, she and Jim were not alone.

Jim gestured toward a chair. "Have a seat, Sally. You know Steve."

She glanced at Steve, sitting rigidly in front of Jim's desk, his tension obvious. Glancing from Jim to Steve, she edged hesitantly to the empty chair and sat. Darby must have talked to Jim.

Jim continued, "We have a problem, and I want to get this cleared up. Steve has something to say to you, Sally." Jim leaned back in his chair, eyeing Steve.

Apprehensive and unsettled, Steve rose and paced across the room, then found sanctuary again in the chair. "As you see, I'm nervous." His eyes pleaded with Sally. "I came in to talk to Jim this morning. I realize that I have a problem, and before I lose this job—a job I enjoy and I'm good at, I told him what I had done. I want to apologize to you, Sally, for what I did at the Renaissance Festival. It was rude and uncalled-for. I treated you badly."

His confession gave Sally a start. Reality struck her. The informer *wasn't* Darby. Trying to understand, Sally studied Steve. "I don't know what to say, Steve. These past couple of years have been bad for me. Apparently, you have some problems yourself."

Steve sat in the chair staring at his shoes. He turned to Sally slowly, his voice a whisper. "I'm an alcoholic, Sally.

I've finally had to face it. I had too much to drink at the Festival, and I've been drinking here at work."

Sally turned to ice. Her hands trembled. Her thoughts tore backward in time, remembering a drunk driver had taken her husband's life. Alcohol destroys people. It destroyed her life, and it was destroying Steve's. For a moment, anger filled her. Then she calmed.

She wanted to punish Steve, telling him about the drunk driver who killed her husband—to make him hurt, the way she had been hurt, but she knew what God wanted her to do. Hurt was not the solution. The answer was love. Forgiveness held a new meaning. "I know it was difficult for you to come in here—to tell Jim and me. I'll pray for your recovery. . .and I forgive you, Steve." The words soared like a weight rising from her shoulders.

Steve's face colored, but for the first time, he looked directly into her eyes. "Thank you, Sally. Believe it or not, I respect you. You don't deserve any more problems in your life. One day I was thinking about you, and I remembered your husband died because of a drunk driver. That reality struck me and knocked some sense into my head. I just wanted you to know that."

Steve stared again at his shoes. "I asked Jim for a leave of absence while I get treatment. I'll succeed. I have to. I can't stand myself anymore."

As his words formed meaning, her heart thudded in her chest. He did know about Tim, and he asked for help. In her act of forgiveness, a calm washed over Sally. Somewhere in her heart, she'd also forgiven the drunk who killed Tim. Though symbolic, the act was complete and sincere. For the first time in over two years, she felt a resolved peace.

Jim came from behind the desk, placing his hand comfortingly on Sally's shoulder as he passed. Steve rose. Jim shook his hand, and taking Steve's arm, he walked with him to the door, talking quietly.

When Steve left the room, Jim returned to Sally. "Thanks. I know this was hard for you, but part of Steve's healing will be to face his problem and ask for forgiveness from those he's hurt."

Sally rose. "I didn't know about his drinking. I should've told you about the situation myself, but I felt guilty for some stupid reason—being a single woman, I suppose. I thought I was another statistic."

"Sally, you were happy as a married woman. Some people aren't meant to be single. I hear a lot of things through the company grapevine, and to be truthful, I'm surprised you didn't accept that young man's proposal. Single women bring out the worst in men."

Sally tensed, and pain shot through her shoulder blades. Was he saying she was partially to blame?

"You belong married. It's safer that way. If I were in your shoes, young lady, I'd pack my bags and run to the arms of that young man of yours. If you don't, some other woman will catch him, and you'll be sorry you let him go."

Sally was startled at his comment and his attitude. She looked at Jim, and all she could think to say was "thank you." She left his office and returned to her desk. The thought of using Brad for security and safety left a bitter taste in her mouth. But to her sadness, his words bore a horrible truth. If she couldn't accept Brad's proposal, someone else would.

sixteen

Brad had dealt restlessly with his final moments with Sally. Her words had shocked him when he left for Providence. Yet he missed her terribly and loved her deeply. After a month settling in, the days dragged and weighed on his spirit. Another month passed as he struggled with indecision. He'd prayed she would call him, but he heard nothing. And if he called, would she hang up? Finally, he blocked his fears and called her. His heart lifted when he heard her voice.

"Is everything all right?"

He heard her concern. "Everything's fine. I needed to hear your voice."

Her tone softened. "It's nice to hear yours. How are the kids?"

"Better than me, I suppose. They like school. Danny's so proud he goes full-time. Kelly loves her teacher. She says she reminds her of. . .you." His voice caught.

After a pause, Sally whispered, "Tell her I think about her every day."

Her words left him frustrated. How could she think of them, yet reject them? He pushed the thought from his mind. "The house is a real family home. So much room for the kids to play." He hoped she heard the word "family." But the house felt empty without her.

"It sounds nice. I'm happy things are going so well."

When he hung up, the call left him drained and empty. But it gave him hope. They had talked. He sent her photographs of the house and the children. But now he felt lonelier than ever before. And a week later, he called again, then two days after that.

"Did you get the photos of the house?"

"Yes, a couple of days ago. It's beautiful. And I love the yard with the gazebo and flowers," she said. "And the kids. They look. . .wonderful." Sadness echoed in her voice.

"We found a church with all kinds of family programs, uplifting worship, and a wonderful Sunday school."

"The kids are in Sunday school, then?"

"They really look forward to Sundays. You should see them."

"I should."

Brad's heart skipped a beat. Did she mean it? "Did I tell you about my neighbors? And my new position?"

"Yes, the last time you called."

Tell her how lonesome you are. He hesitated. "Everything's great, Sally, except one thing. You're in Michigan, and I'm in Rhode Island. I miss you more than I can say. The kids talk about the Cape when you were there, and I was surprised the other day when Kelly remembered the first time she met you. She asked me why she had treated you and Carrie so mean. She's really growing up."

"I know. They grow up too fast." Sadness filled her voice.

"The neighbors remind me of Alice and Ed. Millie and Chet love the kids. It's like having grandparents right next door." He waited for a response, but he heard nothing. "How are Alice and Ed?"

"They're fine. Full of good advice, as always. Sometimes I wonder when I'll listen to them." Her voice trailed off.

Listen to them, Sally, his mind pleaded. "Do you know how much I miss you?" Desperation flooded through him.

"I miss you, too."

Her words lifted him like a flight of swans. "Then come,

Sally. Come for a visit. No pressure, I promise. I'm so anxious for you to see the house. Millie and Chet have a guest room, and they said you were welcome anytime. What do you say? Come for a week, a weekend, a day, just come."

He held his breath, waiting, listening to the lengthening silence.

"Let me think about it, Brad. I'll call you. It would have to be a short visit."

Air shot from his lungs, and his pulse hammered in his temples. "Whatever you can arrange, call me then. I'll take time off. Sally, I can't wait to see you. Please come."

❧

Ridiculous. The single word described Sally's life. Her separation from Brad and the children was absurd. Despite her confusion and fear, she would only be complete when she was with them. She longed to tell Brad what she'd come to realize, but not by telephone. She made arrangements for a trip to Providence for Thanksgiving.

The days straggled along, waiting for the holiday. Only her work and daily responsibilities kept her focused. One afternoon Alice stopped by and asked her to cochair a Mission Project for the Christmas season called the Gift Tree, a clothing and toy drive for children from the County Foster Care Center. Sally readily agreed. Helping to brighten a child's Christmas sounded wonderful, and the activity would fill her lonely, anxious days.

On November 16th, the telephone rang late in the evening. Elaine's husband proudly announced the birth of their son Timothy. He invited her to a celebration party near the Christmas holiday. Sally's invitation to Darby and Eric's December 21st wedding had already arrived, and though she looked forward to the wonderful occasion, she would be alone. Each event helped her pass the time. As Thanksgiving approached,

Sally counted the days until her trip to Providence.

Two days before she was to leave, a different providence came into play. Sally received a distressing call from Beth.

"Sally, Mom died this morning. I wanted you to know."

Sally's heart lay heavy in her chest. "Beth, I'm so sorry."

"She died in her sleep. And, Sally, she really didn't know me any more. She thought I was a nice lady. Occasionally she asked if I were her sister. I could hardly bear to see her that way."

Tears burned in her eyes. "Beth, it's so sad."

"I hate being alone through all of this."

Sally's heavy heart fell and she knew what she had to do. "I'll come to California if you'd like. The holiday is here, and I have the time off. I'll try to get a flight."

"Would you, Sally? I was hoping you'd say you would. I'd love to see you and have you here for a couple of days, anyway."

"I'll make arrangements and call you back, Beth."

Grief for Beth—and for herself—wound through Sally. She longed to see Brad and the kids, but she couldn't leave Beth alone now. The whole situation overtook her. God had to be keeping her and Brad apart, or else, why did this happen now?

Each moment away from Brad made her more certain she was meant to be *with* him, but God was showing her the opposite—that their love wasn't meant to be. With a numb heart, she called the airline, then called Brad and broke the news. Disappointment filled his voice, but he said he understood.

❧

The next day, in a little more than five hours, Sally walked down the gate ramp at the airport.

Beth stood amid the crowd, and when their eyes met, Beth darted forward, throwing her arms around Sally's neck. "I'm so glad you came. It's been so terrible."

She choked back a sob, and Sally held her tightly, and calmed her before they followed the signs to baggage claim.

A half hour drive through heavy traffic led them to Beth's apartment in Santa Monica. Though nondescript, the building stood near the Santa Monica pier and Beth's apartment on the top floor was charming. From the open doors of a small balcony, an occasional ocean breeze drifted through the living room. Sally breathed in the fresh, salty air.

"I've missed you, Sally," Beth said, standing beside her at the balcony door.

"Like old times, Beth. Sometimes I remember when I came to your house to see Tim, and you and I sat together talking and giggling. Tim got so mad at us."

"He did, didn't he? This isn't quite like old times, though. You and I have a lot more problems now than we did then."

"When you're young, everything seems wonderful. I'm really glad I came, Beth. I didn't realize how much I missed you." She wrapped her arm around Beth's shoulder.

"You'll make me cry, Sally," Beth said, wiping away a tear. "I thought we could grab a sandwich, and then go over to the funeral home. I don't expect many visitors, but Mom did have a few old friends and a couple of elderly cousins. The funeral's tomorrow."

"I wish I could've come earlier to help you, Beth."

"You're here now. That's what's important to me."

&

The funeral service was held at the church in Esther Newgate's old neighborhood, and the voice of the pastor echoed in the nearly empty sanctuary. With few mourners and no funeral luncheon, by noon Sally and Beth were seated in a small oceanside café eating salads and looking out at the gray foamy waves dashing on an empty shoreline. The hazy sky offered no hope of sunshine. The sun hid behind the thick, equally gray, cloud cover—a day appropriate for mourning.

Beth, sitting across from Sally, looked up from her salad. "So now, tell me what's really going on in your life."

Sally stared at her plate. The past year flew through her mind. The ups and downs, the positives and negatives. What would Beth say? Could Sally bear to hear Beth's possible biting words about Brad? Yet she'd hid things far too long.

Sally looked out at the empty beach and then back at Beth. "A lot and nothing. How's that for an ambiguous response?"

Beth scowled, obviously confused.

Sally sighed. "I have so many things inside me, I don't know where to begin."

"Start at the beginning, as the song goes."

With Beth's full attention, Sally told her about Brad and the children, the proposal, and Brad's promotion and move to Rhode Island.

Beth's eyes widened. "Sally, I'm thrilled for you. I've waited to hear this wonderful news. But I don't understand your hesitation. Don't you love him?"

Her response shot through Sally like a cannon. Of all the people who should feel differently, it was Beth. Her pulse tripped through her veins. "Yes, I do—and the kids. But we've only known each other a year. I felt so lonely after Tim died, and then Brad stepped into my life. I don't know if I can trust my feelings. Sometimes I feel God doesn't want us together. And I've struggled with leaving Michigan. Moving to Rhode Island means leaving my home, my family, my friends, my job. It means leaving the years I had with Tim. It means taking a chance." Her voice faded to a whisper.

Beth leaned forward, her hands knotted in front of her. "So, what's happening now?"

"That's where the *nothing* comes in. Nothing. I'm doing

nothing. Brad moved and started a new life in Providence and I am just sitting in Michigan."

"But why? Why are you doing that? If you love him and his kids, why wouldn't you marry him? Would God have brought the two of you together if He didn't want you to fall in love?"

"I felt that way at first. But so many people cautioned me about the illusions of new romances. A year isn't very long. I've been afraid."

"Time doesn't measure love, Sally. Don't miss out on a new, wonderful life. I'm Tim's sister. I should be the first to protect the memory of my brother's marriage. But Sally, Tim is gone. Here's a man, living and breathing, who loves you and wants to marry you. And his children love you. If you love him, don't hold back for other people. Your friends are your friends. Your family's your family. Sally, you and I rarely see each other, and yet it doesn't diminish our relationship."

Sally heard her words and remembered hearing them so long ago. How had she forgotten them?

Beth touched her hand. "We still love and care about each other. Bill and Sue and Carrie will never stop loving you if you move. They're family. But, Sally, how long can you love someone long-distance with no commitment? Brad may love you deeply, but if you don't love him enough to go to him, how long do you expect him to wait for a dream? If God's given you another chance for love and happiness, take the gift. Don't let it go."

Beth had touched on the heart of the matter, and her words rang in Sally's ears. Though Sally's fears were foolish, they were real. She loved Beth for opening her eyes and her heart. Had she closed them to God's wishes, too? Now, she would deal with them, and Beth was right. How much longer would Brad wait?

&

A smile spread across Brad's face simply hearing Sally's voice. As they talked about the funeral and their lonely Thanksgivings, what he really wanted to talk about was them.

"So when will I see you, Sally?"

"Soon. I've done a lot of thinking, and we really need to talk, but face-to-face, not on the telephone."

A chill ran through him. "Is something wrong?"

"No, nothing's wrong. We've been through so much, and I feel. . .I guess, I'd rather be together when we talk."

"The Christmas holiday's coming."

"I know. That's what I'd hoped, and I can't wait. I talked to Ed. He has room for you, and the kids can stay here with me. What do you say?"

She bubbled her plans, and disappointment flooded through him. "Sally, I can't. I'm visiting Mom on the Cape. As always, she's prepared her usual calendar of activities. And I'd planned to ask you to join us when you came for Thanksgiving. I'm anxious for you to see the new house, but that can wait. It's you I want to see. Can't you go with us to the Cape?"

Before she spoke, he knew her response from the long, uncomfortable pause. He froze. Were empty promises and weeks apart all their relationship had to offer?

"Brad, I can't stand this any more. Nothing works out. I have the party for Elaine's new baby and I'm going to Darby's wedding. And the mission project with Alice, remember? I can't let her down again. She's done so much for me."

"I suppose. What's another month or two?" Frustration and sarcasm sounded in his ears. "You know, Sally, I've tried to be patient. I'm sorry."

"I'm sorry, too."

When Brad hung up, he sat in silence. Sally had drifted

further and further from him. Fear sent an icy chill through his veins, freezing his heart. He'd reached the end of patience. His love wasn't enough to make her love him in return. And the children. Dragging things on would only hurt them more. It had to end.

He sank into a chair and stared through the window at the leafless trees and the death of summer. He was through. No more. No matter what. The pain hurt too much.

seventeen

The phone call with Brad left Sally devastated. She'd pushed him to the limit. She'd been thoughtless, filling her calendar with commitments without thinking of him. At first, everything seemed to keep them apart—people's comments, Kelly's jealousy, schedules, job promotions, but, mostly, her own fears.

She had been praying daily for reassurance that Brad was the man God meant for her. But Beth's words were true. Why would God lead her to Brad if there was no reason? For the first time in months, she felt determined. She faced it head on. *I love this man with all my heart. I love his children. I want to be his wife. I want. . .*

Sally stopped and listened, listened to the deafening silence. She looked around the room at what had been her home for many years. She realized her life was missing something—nothing material, nothing she could buy. She was missing the man she loved. It wasn't too late. Her heart told her everything would be fine. She would visit Brad *before* Christmas and tell him she loved him and wanted to be his wife. Everything would be wonderful.

She hesitated. Should she call him tonight? She breathed deeply and dialed Brad's number, praying she'd hear jubilation when she told him.

She heard the click, and Brad's hello.

Her heart thundered. "Brad—"

"Please, Sally, don't apologize. You're right."

She froze. *Right?* She was wrong. Absolutely wrong. "But—"

"Sally, please don't say anything else."

She clung to the telephone, her breath like ice burning through her. The pause grew in length.

"I've been thinking since we hung up, Sally. And you're right. I've been beating my head against the wall, praying and hoping. But I don't want to drag this on any longer. We've both had enough of stress and empty hopes."

Gooseflesh covered Sally's arms, her knees buckled beneath her. She grabbed the edge of the table and sank into the nearby chair. "No, Brad, no. I've been thinking. I wanted to talk to you when we're together. I. . ."

"You've been thinking for a long time, Sally. Talking and thinking isn't the solution. Loving is. I don't think our love is strong enough to carry us through all of the problems. You made me see things clearly. I was blinded by my feelings. But you've said it all, Sally. It's over. I can't bear to go through this anymore. No more promises or wishes or talking."

A growing lump pressed against Sally's vocal chords, allowing nothing but silence. Her chest ached with the pressure of her thundering heartbeat, the pain knifing down into her stomach. She hung her head, tears dripping on her hands and running across her paled lips. "It's over?" she finally asked in a whisper.

"It's for the best. For both of us. And for the kids."

The empty line stretched into dead silence. A whispered good-bye left her lips, and her trembling hand placed the receiver back onto the cradle. She raised her icy fingers to her face and wept until her tears dried to racking sobs.

She wandered into the bedroom, tossing her clothes in a pile and pulled a nightgown over her head. She lay across the bed, fighting the tears that again burned on the edges of her eyes. Why had she been such a fool?

Her ear was tuned for the telephone, praying he'd rescind

and call her back. She surveyed the objects around the room, things that meant nothing without Brad. When her gaze drifted to the nightstand, she spotted her Bible, unopened for months. She remembered the day with embarrassment when she had asked Ed if he attended church. His answer was candid and insightful. *No, but I read my Bible every night before I go to bed. It gives me perspective.* That's what she had missed. Somehow along the way, she had lost perspective.

Sally rose on her elbow and grasped the Bible in her hand. She opened it, turning to Jack's lessons from her grief group, Ecclesiastes 3:1. Glancing at the page, she carried the Bible into the living room. She leaned her back against the chair, staring at the page in front of her, running her fingers across the black leather binding of the book. Her eyes focused on the passage. *To everything there is a season, and a time to every purpose under the heaven: a time to be born, and a time to die.* "A time to be born and a time to die." The words tore through her. Yes, death was also a season. She searched the page. *A time to heal; a time to break down, and a time to build up; a time to weep, and a time to laugh; a time to mourn, and a time to dance.*

She'd experienced all of these feelings. She had mourned and wept. With Brad, she had healed and laughed. And her heart had danced. She again focused her eyes on the page. *A time to get, and a time to lose.* But this couldn't be her time to lose. She'd already lost Tim. She didn't want to throw away the love she felt for Brad and the children. She had taken so long to realize the truth. With them, her lonely life was full and complete. A new tear formed on the rim of her eye. And she sought the words. *A time to speak; A time to love.*

Sally looked up from her reading. Her throat tightened. Her heart pounded in her chest. Here was the answer she had sought all along. God had given her the seasons of her life, and she had faced them. She reread the words. *To everything there is a season, and a time to every purpose under the heaven.* How could she question God's purpose for her? She had been given a loving man who wanted her for a wife. And two beautiful children—children she'd longed for—needing a nurturing woman in their lives.

Sally placed the Bible on the table and rose from the chair, crossing to the telephone. God had answered her prayer. The problem was she hadn't listened. She hit the redial button. The telephone rang. Three rings. . .four. . .five. . . No one answered. She looked at her wristwatch. Ten o'clock. The children would be in bed by now. He had to be home. Reality struck her. Brad knew she was calling back, and he didn't answer the telephone.

She placed the receiver on the cradle. She felt dizzy, and her heart ached. Shaken and weak, she fled to her bedroom. Flinging herself on the bed, tears flowed, burning down her cheeks. *Heavenly Father, I've fought You. I haven't listened to Your message. I've blamed You, and all the while, You were handing me a gift and I had my eyes closed. Forgive me. You've opened my eyes to Your will.* She closed her eyes, whispering her prayer until she fell asleep.

❧

All those things that seemed so important marched past Sally like a blur—Darby's wedding and the party for baby Timothy. She worked on the mission project, and on Christmas Eve Day, the packages were delivered to the County Foster Care Center. Her heart ached seeing the parentless children, and their image blurred into the sweet faces of Kelly and Danny.

One surprise arrived as a Christmas card. The return address caught her eye, Old Wharf Road, Dennisport. The handwriting, precise and flowing, was familiar, and she knew it was from Amanda.

With trembling fingers, Sally tore open the letter. It began casually with the typical Christmas greeting. Amanda thanked her again for the lovely vase Sally sent last summer and wrote about her Thanksgiving visit with Brad.

> *I was sorry you could not be with us for Thanks-*
> *giving. It was wonderful to be with Brad and the*
> *children, but I sensed that things are not as joyful as*
> *they were when they were on the Cape last summer. I*
> *must attribute that to your absence. I do not want to*
> *be a meddling old lady, but I felt you and Brad had a*
> *relationship based on mutual respect and caring for*
> *one another. Therefore, I do not understand why Brad*
> *is alone in Providence, and you are alone in Michigan.*

Sally's hands trembled as she scanned the ivory stationary. The words blurred in her eyes.

> *Despite all my concerns, I respect your reason, what-*
> *ever it may be, not to accept my son's proposal. You*
> *brought much happiness into the lives of Brad and the*
> *children, and I thank you for that. I ask you to forgive*
> *an old woman's meddling. I wish you blessings and*
> *much peace and happiness in your life.*
>
> > *Fondly,*
> > *Amanda*

Sally sat unmoving, staring at the letter. *You aren't med-dling, Amanda. You really love me and you love your family.* Pangs of shame swept through her. Kelly and Danny needed her to care for them and love them. She could never replace Janet, but she could love them. And she did.

Brad had not told Amanda about their terrible, final con-versation, and she grasped onto that piece of information with hope. She hoped he would call her, but the hoped-for call didn't happen.

After Christmas Eve worship service, Alice and Ed arrived, smiling foolishly, with a package under Ed's arm. Before they were seated, Sally couldn't contain her question. "So, what's all the grinning about?"

Ed wrapped his free arm around Alice's shoulder. "I've asked Alice to be my wife, and she accepted."

"God's blessed us a second time," Alice said. "I never thought I'd marry again and neither did Ed, but we enjoy each other's company, we share the same faith, and best of all, we love each other." Ed leaned down, kissing her gently.

Sally stared at them in wonder. "I'm thrilled." Yet, her happiness for them was stifled by her own self-pity. She looked from one to the other, still standing in the foyer. "I suppose I can invite you to sit down now."

They laughed as they moved to the living room. But before they were seated, Ed, as eager as a child, plopped a gift into Sally's arms.

Sally eyed the package. "What is this?"

"You'd know if you opened it," Ed said, a twinkle in his eye.

"Okay, but help yourself to some cookies and coffee." She pointed to the table covered in a red and green cloth and filled with Christmas goodies.

With the first turn of the package, Sally heard a tinkle from inside. "It's a music box, isn't it?" She tore off the paper. When she raised the lid, her heart skipped a beat. A miniature castle with turrets and towers stood on top of the music box, and winding the key, the castle turned, sending out the airy melody "Someday My Prince Will Come." She hadn't told them of her situation with Brad. Tears crept into her eyes.

Alice's knowing gaze rested on her. "You can't be sad, Sally. Your prince has already come. We love you dearly, but we wanted to say something. You need to be in Providence. There's a man and two children who love you very much. You'll move away, and we'll visit you. Distance doesn't end friendships. But distance ends romance."

Sally looked at the two of them. Her eyes glistened with tears—too many tears lately. She held the lovely music box in her hand. "It's too late. I finally realized I can't live here anymore without Brad and the kids. But I've messed things up badly."

Alice rose and walked to Sally's side. Like a mother, she turned Sally's face to hers. "Have faith, my dear. I'm sure you haven't."

Sally was sure she had, but how could she explain the whole thing to Alice?

&

On Christmas Day after worship, Sally forced herself to prepare dinner as she'd planned. Sally lit the logs in the fireplace, and as the fire reached a rosy glow, she heard a car in the driveway. In seconds, the front door burst open, and Carrie ran into the room, throwing her arms around Sally's waist. Bill, Sue, and her parents from Florida followed close behind as Sally met them at the door.

Hiding her feelings through the hugs and Christmas salutations, Sally used the meal to keep herself busy, and she controlled the emotion building inside her.

After dinner, Sue and Sally cleared the dishes and stored the leftovers while the others visited in the living room. Carrie brought along a new game, and as Grandma Meier read the rules at the gateleg table, Carrie played with the music box. Its tinkling tune played again and again. The sound drifted into the kitchen.

"If I hear that tune one more time. . ." Sue said, scurrying to the living room.

As Sally prepared the coffee, Bill wandered into the kitchen, and she grabbed the moment. Despite what had happened between her and Brad, she had to let Bill know how much his words had hurt her. "Sit down for a minute, Bill. I need to talk to you."

He tilted his head in question and slid uncomfortably into a chair. "What's up?"

"This is important. I know you weren't happy about my relationship with Brad. And I'm sure you were relieved when he moved away. Things are probably hopeless now, but you should know that I love Brad and his kids."

Bill raised his hand to halt her speech. "Listen, Sis, you don't have to explain your life to me. Maybe I was a fool. You haven't been the same since he left. A couple of years ago we expected you to be depressed and lonely. Then you seemed happier again, but now all you do is moon around. That's not a life. I want you to be happy."

She looked directly into his eyes. "Brad proposed last summer and I refused because I didn't want to leave Michigan— my family and friends, my job. But I've been miserable. I listened to so many people cautioning me, telling me my relationship with Brad was too new to mean anything. I was so caught up in my own worries I didn't even listen to God. Now that I realize my foolishness, it's too late. I'll never listen to anyone again, Bill—except my heart and God."

Bill looked at her in silence. "I'm sorry, Sis. I didn't mean to hurt you. I thought I was protecting you, but I was probably being selfish. I didn't give him or your relationship a chance. Your happiness is all I care about."

He rose and Sally stepped into his arms, her head on his shoulder. "Thanks. If I have another chance with Brad, I'll not refuse again. I love him too much, and I believe he and the kids are what God planned for me." She took him by the hand.

"So, come into the living room with me. I want to tell everyone the news. Last night, Alice and Ed told me they're getting married. And if God gives me another chance, so will I."

❧

Brad carried the dinner dishes into the kitchen. As always, his mother had given Naomi Christmas Day off to be with her family. They had warmed the turkey Naomi prepared the day before in its deep brown gravy. Their meal seemed quiet. The children ate slowly, tired from the excitement of gifts and special treats. Amanda eyed him throughout the meal, obviously knowing he wasn't himself.

When Brad talked to Sally before Christmas, he knew then she didn't love him as he loved her. Though her words of love seemed real, her actions spoke differently. She filled her life with commitments, never once thinking of him. Then maybe he did the same.

But he couldn't bear the pain anymore, not for himself nor the children. She meant too much to them. That's why her words had cut him deeply when she called the last time. He felt as if he were an afterthought. Now he knew he'd let foolish pride destroy their relationship. Life would never be right if he didn't try one last time.

With thoughts chasing through his head, he rinsed the dinner dishes, and grabbing a cup of coffee, he returned to the living room where Amanda read to the children. Brad sat in a chair, listening to his mother like he did when he was a child, and pondered what to do.

Her voice jolted him from his wandering thoughts. "Did you hear me, Brad?" She held a stack of Christmas cards in her lap. The children had gone to their rooms to get ready for bed without him noticing.

"Sorry, Mom. I guess I was thinking."

She nodded, her eyes reflecting her concern. "Did you

read Darlene's card?"

He shook his head no.

"She is going with a very nice man, she says in her note. They are talking about marriage. She sounds very happy."

"I'm glad. She deserves to be happy." His voice sounded bitter, and he flinched.

Amanda tossed the cards on the end table. "Brad, what are you going to do? You cannot continue on like this. You've been in a terrible state far too long."

"I know. I want her, Mom. But I told her it was over."

"You did what?"

"It's a long story, but I told her on the telephone, we were through. Her indecision hurt too much. I couldn't take it anymore, and I worried for the children. They've grown to love her."

"Yes, they talk about her all the time."

"I didn't tell them. I didn't have the courage."

"Brad, you must do something."

"I thought telling her would end it, but I love her."

"I'd hoped you and Sally would marry. Whatever you do, be decisive. This has gone on long enough."

Brad rose from the chair. "You're right. I know what I have to do."

eighteen

Sally rose the morning after Christmas feeling as if she'd carried heavy loads up a hill, over and over. Her body ached, and her heart ached. She struggled into her robe. This Christmas seemed worse than when Tim died. Death was forever. Brad and the children were only distanced by earthly miles. If they loved each other, miles should make no difference.

She wandered into the kitchen and made coffee then carried it to the living room. She sat in the recliner, staring at the unlit tree and the pile of neatly stacked gifts beneath it.

How could she expect Brad to wait? Why had she allowed foolish fears and worries to control her decision? She had expected God's assurance to stomp through in heavy boots. Brad had reminded her that sometimes God can answer prayer softly. Her mind had been so filled with fear, she hadn't heard the Lord's soft, gentle assurance.

Sally sat back in her chair, staring out the window. Fluffy white flakes drifted down, swaying and looping on the wind, pressing against the windowpane and melting into tiny rivulets of water like tears. She watched one float on the air, drift down, and cling to the branches of a shrub outside her window. She felt like that snowflake, drifting and clinging. Where was her faith?

She returned to the kitchen, pouring a fresh cup of coffee and toasting an English muffin. She sat at the table, staring at the snow. God had been with her all along. In her struggle, she had forgotten to trust in the Lord, to know that God guided her steps.

The snow floated down, heavier now, and lay on the branches

of the shrubs, no longer clinging, but resting on the limbs. She had been clinging to fear and sadness, but no more. Today, she rested on God's promise, on the Lord's assurance.

Finishing the simple breakfast, she showered and dressed. There was no point in calling Brad today. She'd give him time. In a few days, she'd call him, then go to him—plead with him. She couldn't give up. It took her this long to hear God, not in the blare of trumpets, but in a gentle whisper.

She returned to the living room and lifted the Bible, seeking the solace. The snow slowed and finally stopped. She rose from the chair, needing to do something invigorating. Throwing on her coat, Sally headed outside, strengthened by the icy air as the Word strengthened her spirit.

Before she stepped from the back porch, the telephone rang, and her heart leaped. *Brad*. She rushed inside and snatched the receiver, only to hear Ed's nervous voice.

"Sally, would you come down for a minute?"

"Is something wrong?"

"No, nothing's wrong, but I need to see you. Could you come down now?"

Her chest tightened. Something was wrong. "What is it?"

"Just come down, Sally."

His persistence concerned her. He and Alice broke their engagement. Or something as bad. He didn't want to tell her on the telephone. "I'll be there."

Hurrying back outside, she raced down the block, and as she climbed Ed's porch, he opened the door.

"What's wrong, Ed?" she gasped as she stepped in. He looked at her strangely. It was bad news. He took her coat and laid it on the chair near the door.

"Go into the living room. I'll be there in a minute." He turned down the hall toward the kitchen.

Her mind raced. What could it be? She turned into the living room, and in the dusky light of the snowy morning, her eyes were captured by the colorful lights from a small tabletop tree reflecting in the windowpane. The colors diffused like fireworks. She turned toward a chair, then stopped. Her heart thundered, and she couldn't believe her eyes. "Brad! You're here."

Brad saw Sally coming up the walk, her face pale and drawn. But when she saw him, her face glowed, and she raced into his arms, clinging to him, trembling. His own heart beat next to hers, his own tears flowed with hers.

"Brad, I can't believe you're here. I wanted to see you so badly. I needed to. . ."

He leaned down, silencing her with his lips. Her own lips yielded to his, breath bursting from their lungs as they parted.

Her eyes searched his. "I don't understand. I'm so happy you're here, but. . .I don't understand."

Brad led her to the sofa. He sat her down, sitting next to her. "I made a decision, Sally. I don't want to lose you. I love you and need you. The kids love you. Even my mother loves you. I'm here to beg you from the bottom of my heart to give our love a chance."

Sally laughed and cried at the same time. "Please, Brad, don't say anymore. I was so afraid I lost you. When I finally came to my senses, you told me we were through. I thought it was too late."

"It's not too late. I love you too much." He encircled her in his arms, looking down into her tearstained face, tears brimming in his own eyes. "Sally, I don't have enough words to tell you the feelings inside me. You make my life complete. And you bring joy to the children. Will you marry me?"

She grasped his hands with her icy, trembling fingers. Her eyes said everything he needed to hear. "Yes, I'll marry you.

I love you with all my heart."

He held her to him, shaking with relief and the depth of his love. Her eyes, though teary, glowed with happiness. "I love you, your children—and your mother." A smile spread across her face, relaxing the stress, and Brad's own tense mouth curled to a grin.

Applause resounded from the hall. Alice and Ed peeked around the corner, beaming with their own joy. They rushed into the room with kisses and handshakes. When the congratulations subsided, Sally sank exhausted on the sofa. "Someone, please explain this whole thing to me. Where are the children? When did you get here? How long—"

"Slow down, my love." He took her hand in his. "I'll explain everything, but first, I want to give you your Christmas present. It's long overdue."

He raised a package from the end table and handed it to her. She looked at him with question and unwrapped the box. When she lifted the lid, she brought out a beautiful leaded-glass box decorated with pressed flowers. "Oh, Brad, it's the box I saw on the Cape—the antique box I loved so much."

"Open it, Sally."

She lifted the lid. Inside was a smaller, hinged jewelry box. She glanced at him, then raising the lid, she smiled. She held her arms out to him, and he wrapped her in his arms, knowing that his prayers had been answered.

He released her and, taking the box, lifted out a glimmering solitaire diamond ring.

"Brad, it's beautiful!" He lifted her left hand and slid on the ring, threading his fingers through hers.

"You see, dear," Alice said, "it fits. It's amazing what I can find out when I need to."

Sally glanced down at the ring, fitting perfectly on her finger.

"Alice, you knew this all along?"

"He bought the ring long ago, my dear. He's been waiting for you to say yes."

Sally wiped her moist eyes.

"Now, to answer your questions," Brad began. "The kids are with my mom. I flew out standby last night. I thought it would take forever."

"This is like a dream. Does your mom know about—"

"They all know why I'm here. Mom's overjoyed. Kelly and Danny are thrilled, and they are all praying that you will say yes."

"But, Brad, why didn't you tell me you were coming? I called you back the night of our argu—of our talk and you didn't pick up the phone. I thought you were avoiding me. I—"

"We went out after your call. I couldn't bear to sit in the house. I really thought you didn't love me. Then, I decided to try one last time. I called Alice late last night. I knew you talked with her, and I wanted to know the truth."

He glanced at Alice's glowing face, and she nodded. "She assured me that you loved me and you'd accept my proposal. So I rushed to the airport and waited for a flight. I needed to ask you in person, not by telephone."

She put her hands to her face, laughing and crying. But he knew the tears were joyful. Embracing her, he kissed her hair and pressed his cheek against hers. He felt lightheaded—giddy. He leaned back, tilting her face toward his, their eyes glazed with love. "When I asked you, I wanted to look into your eyes."

Sally's heart overflowed. "And you are," she whispered. Her mind ruffled through the pages of their lives the past months. Today she felt complete, filled with love and faith. She rose, taking his hands in hers, and tugging him upward. "Now, let's telephone the children."

SCONES (Griddle Cakes)

Here are the scones that Sally made for her neighbor Ed Washburn. They are cooked on a black iron griddle, heavy fry pan, or electric fry pan.

1 ½ teaspoon baking powder
½ teaspoon salt
½ teaspoon ground ginger
2 cups all-purpose flour (plus extra for dusting)
½ cup granulated sugar
¾ cup unsalted butter, cut into small pieces.
1 cup sultanas (golden raisins) or any dried fruit, such as cherries, cranberries, or diced apricot.
2 large eggs
3–4 teaspoons milk

Sift dry ingredients in bowl and stir in sugar. Rub butter until the mixture is like fine bread crumbs. Stir in the dried fruit. Beat the eggs and add them. Stir in just enough milk to make a firm but sticky dough. Turn the dough onto a floured board, sprinkle with flour and roll it to a ½ inch thickness. Cut into rounds. Re-roll the trimmings and cut more rounds. Brush heavy fry pan with oil and heat over medium. Fry cakes for about 5 minutes on each side until they are well browned. Serve warm with butter or preserves. Also good plain. You may store and eat them cold as well.

A Letter To Our Readers

Dear Reader:

In order that we might better contribute to your reading enjoyment, we would appreciate your taking a few minutes to respond to the following questions. When completed, please return to the following:

Rebecca Germany, Managing Editor
Heartsong Presents
PO Box 719
Uhrichsville, Ohio 44683

1. Did you enjoy reading *Seasons?*
   ❑ Very much. I would like to see more books
      by this author!
   ❑ Moderately
      I would have enjoyed it more if _____

   _____

2. Are you a member of **Heartsong Presents**? ❑Yes ❑No
   If no, where did you purchase this book?_____

   _____

3. What influenced your decision to purchase this
   book? (Check those that apply.)

   ❑ Cover   ❑ Back cover copy

   ❑ Title   ❑ Friends

   ❑ Publicity   ❑ Other_____

4. How would you rate, on a scale from 1 (poor) to 5
   (superior), the cover design? _____

5. On a scale from 1 (poor) to 10 (superior), please rate the following elements.

___Heroine   ___Plot

___Hero   ___Inspirational theme

___Setting   ___Secondary characters

6. What settings would you like to see covered in **Heartsong Presents** books?_____

_____

_____

7. What are some inspirational themes you would like to see treated in future books?_____

_____

_____

8. Would you be interested in reading other **Heartsong Presents** titles?   ❏ Yes   ❏ No

9. Please check your age range:
   ❏ Under 18   ❏ 18-24   ❏ 25-34
   ❏ 35-45   ❏ 46-55   ❏ Over 55

10. How many hours per week do you read? _____

Name _____

Occupation_____

Address_____

City____ _____ State_____ Zip _____

Most holidays last only a short while,

but the romance of Christmas lingers on. It is the season for mistletoe and crackling fires, for stolen kisses and ecstatic reunions, for blushing glances and the heart-pounding magic of love. Recapture the wonder of Christmas in these two brand new four-in-one novella collections.

Remember Christmases long gone past in *A Nostalgic Noel*—featuring *Kay Cornelius, Rebecca Germany, Darlene Mindrup,* and *Colleen L. Reece.*

Celebrate today with *Season of Love*—featuring *Yvonne Lehman, Lorree Lough, Tracie Peterson,* and *Debra White Smith.*

Both: Trade Paperback, 352 Pages

Please send me____copies of *A Nostalgic Noel* and ____copies of *Season of Love.* I am enclosing $4.97 each. (Please add $1.00 to cover postage and handling per order. OH add 6% tax.)
Send check or money order, no cash or C.O.D.s please.

Name_____

Address _____

City, State, Zip _____

To place a credit card order, call 1-800-847-8270.
Send to: Heartsong Presents Reader Service,
PO Box 719, Uhrichsville, OH 44683

Hearts♥ng Presents
Love Stories Are Rated G!

That's for godly, gratifying, and of course, great! If you love a thrilling love story, but don't appreciate the sordidness of some popular paperback romances, **Heartsong Presents** is for you. In fact, **Heartsong Presents** is the *only inspirational romance book club*, the only one featuring love stories where Christian faith is the primary ingredient in a marriage relationship.

Sign up today to receive your first set of four, never before published Christian romances. Send no money now; you will receive a bill with the first shipment. You may cancel at any time without obligation, and if you aren't completely satisfied with any selection, you may return the books for an immediate refund!

Imagine. . .four new romances every four weeks—two historical, two contemporary—with men and women like you who long to meet the one God has chosen as the love of their lives. . .all for the low price of $9.97 postpaid.

To join, simply complete the coupon below and mail to the address provided. **Heartsong Presents** romances are rated G for another reason: They'll arrive *Godspeed!*

Jack opened the meeting with prayer and introduced his topic, "A Time to Seek."

Brad felt rattled by Sally's nearness. He recalled about nine months after Janet died, his cousin Darlene invited him to dinner. She hadn't told him she'd also invited a divorced lady friend. He'd made the best he could out of the situation, but in his heart, the evening was a disaster. At work, women dropped hints here and there they were available and interested. The problem was, he wasn't—until now.

Concentrating on the presentation proved difficult. Brad couldn't keep his eyes from Sally. She followed Jack's every move. Her expression reflected Jack's words, her head nodding, her mouth curving into a fleeting grin.

Suddenly, she turned toward Brad with a questioning glance, her skin tone rising to a shy schoolgirl pink. Tender sensations surged through him. Before he could force his attention on Jack, the presentation concluded.

"Jack's right," Sally said. "It's what you said. You can't sit around waiting for life to happen, you have to find a new life, make new friends and new traditions. Sounds easier than it is." She rose, and Brad followed.

"I couldn't help but think of my cousin's good intentions at playing matchmaker. A horrible experience. I wasn't ready at all. Haven't been, yet. Not one date."

Sally's eyes brightened. "Nice to know I'm not alone—and it's been longer for me. A coworker asked me to dinner, and you'd think he asked me to eat worms. I panicked. I disappointed myself."

"Maybe he wasn't the right one." His pulse fluttered as a faint ray of hope rose inside him. "One day it'll happen for both of us." He gazed into her lovely eyes, and his mind filled with images. *Maybe someday you'll like to have dinner with me.*

GAIL GAYMER MARTIN is native to the Detroit, Michigan area. A retired high school teacher of English and speech and, later, a guidance counselor, Gail presently is on the adjunct teaching staff in the English curriculum at Detroit College of Business. Though she has written most of her life, Gail began to write professionally in 1995. Besides her novels, she writes parenting articles, Sunday school materials, and is the author of six worship resource books. She is also a contributing editor of *The Christian Communicator*.

To my husband, Bob. With my deepest love and thanks. Your love and support is my season and purpose under heaven. And in memory of my dad, W. Frank Gaymer who is smiling down from heaven and singing with the angels.

Praise and thanks to God for giving me my dream. Thanks to Mom (my greatest fan), family, and friends who have had confidence in my ability and listened to my long stories about writing. Much thanks goes to Gina, my fellow novelist and critique partner, who offered so many helpful suggestions. Thanks also to Terry, friend and fellow novelist, for your support. Thanks to my church friends who tackled the novel in its infancy: Lil and Grace, and to Susan Titus Osborn at The Christian Communicator Manuscript Critique Service. Her professional guidance was the beginning of my growth as a novelist. And